perfect
love
story

NATASHA
MADISON

Cover Design: Melissa Gill with MGBookCovers & Designs

Book formatting CP Smith
Editing done by Jenny Sims Editing for Indies
Proofing Julie Deaton Author Services by Julie Deaton

Dedication

Erica may you find your perfect love story and may he treat you like the princess you are! (when you're 30) I love you!

Chapter One
Hailey

"Hello." Turning down "Glorious" by Macklemore blasting in the background while I washed the kitchen floor with Pine Sol and water, I answer the phone after the first ring.

"It's me." I hear my best friend and cousin, Crystal, say from the other end. "Where are you?" I can't see her face, but I know something is wrong. Even though she's asked me that question a million times before, this time it's different. There is no carefree tone. This time, it's curt and to the point with no laughter in her voice.

"I'm home," I say, almost whispering as my hand shakes against my ear. My mouth suddenly goes dry, my neck starting to get hot. Something inside my stomach suddenly drops when a slow burn sets in.

"You need to come to the hospital." Crystal is an emergency room nurse at St. Mary's, so whatever feeling I was having before has now doubled. "Blake is on his way to get you." When she mentions my brother, I now know something is gravely wrong. The honk outside doesn't allow me to question her any further. "You need to get in the car, okay?" she says softly but firmly. "Listen to me, Hailey. Go outside and get here." My head nods as the hand holding my phone to my ear falls away.

The front door opens, and Blake comes in, looking at me with sorrow and sadness. His brown eyes meet mine briefly, and then he looks down. He doesn't say anything to me; he simply holds out his hand to me. I put my hand in his, and he leads me out to his truck. He opens the door for me, helping me take that step in.

As I'm looking at him, he pulls the seat belt over my chest and buckles me in. My mind's still playing the phone call, trying to dissect the conversation. Trying to find one little word that can be the clue. "It's going to be okay." His voice breaks through the haze.

I nod my head at him, then he steps back and shuts the door, jogging over to his side. He gets in and puts the truck in drive. I'm on the outside looking in, watching my life fall apart without knowing it.

The only thing I'm certain of is that the sun is shining without a cloud in the sky. As I watch a bird soar through the sky almost in the same direction we are going, I think to myself, *Bad things don't happen when it's sunny outside, right?*

I watch the bird, not even realizing we've made it to the hospital. I don't have a chance to open my door because Blake has it opened before I even think to reach for the handle. "You're going to be okay," he assures me as he raises his baseball cap to run his hands through his short dark hair.

"What's going on?" I have feeling my entire life is about to change, so I beg him to tell me before we walk through those doors. Blake doesn't answer. He just reaches down to grab my hand and lead me through the revolving doors.

The harsh smell of antiseptic immediately fills my nose. Voices bombard me, though, none of them are familiar. Glancing around, I take in the hustle and bustle of the emergency room. My heartbeat echoes in my ears as I try in vain to locate a familiar face. I just need to know who we're here for.

As we silently walk down the corridor, my mind never stops thinking about why we are here. I look up at Blake, asking the one question that makes my heart squeeze with such intense pain, it feels like it might explode.

"Is it Mom? Dad?" I can hear the pleading in my tone. He gives me nothing, continuing to look straight ahead. My eyes go back to the floor, following the tile pattern as we make our way beyond the entrance to the emergency room. The first thing I see is both of my parents, alive and healthy. My mother has tears running down her cheeks, and my father has his arm around her shoulders. They are standing next to the nurses' station. I look back at Blake in horror. "Is it Nanny?"

He doesn't have time to answer because Crystal comes out from behind the nurses' station in her everyday uniform of blue scrubs and Crocs, wearing a stethoscope around her neck.

With one glance at her face, I stop my feet in their tracks. My feet are stuck to the floor as if someone crazy glued them to that spot. I can see the hurt and tears in her eyes. She looks at me with her head tilted sideways, her bottom lip trembling. My body blocks any movements I try to make. I try to advance to Crystal, but I can't. My knees start to give out, and a horrible shrieking sound comes from somewhere.

I try turning my head to see where the yelling is coming from, but I can't. I'm on my hands and knees in the hospital corridor. It isn't until the coldness seeps through my hands that I realize I'm the one screaming. That wretched sound is coming from me. *Me*. My throat raw, my eyes burning, and my heart irrevocably broken. No words need to be said. No confirmation given. I don't need them to bring me to a place where we can "talk quietly." It's at that moment I finally know what everyone else knows.

My husband is dead.

My brother bends to pick me up, my body enveloped by his warmth. He carries me to the little white room I didn't want to enter. He sets me on a chair, and my father's strong, warm arms wrap around me. I rest my head on his shoulder while my mother takes a seat on my other side. My father cradles me in his arms. Pieces of conversations float around me as I try to come to grips with the life-changing news.

"It was a head-on collison."

"He was DOA."

I turn in my father's arms and ask in a hoarse voice, "Where is he?" I try to stand, my legs still weak.

"Honey," my father says as he stands up with me, putting his arm around my shoulder to give me the strength to remain standing. "I don't think …"

"I need to see him." I can hear the resolve in my tone. I *need* this. I look at Crystal, who can see my determination in my eyes. My best friend nods and holds out her hand to me. I put my hand in hers, and the strength in her grip gives me the push I need.

"I have to warn you …" She doesn't have time to say anything else because, at that moment, two officers walk into the waiting room. They look around, and once their eyes fall on me, they freeze. Frank Vincent, one of the officers, and I went to high school together. I can see the pity on his face as his eyes meet mine.

He takes his hat off as he makes his way to me with a brown bag in his hand. "Hailey. I'm so, so sorry for your loss." I don't know what to say, so I just nod. "Here are Eric's belongings from the scene." He hands me the small brown bag folded at the top, weighing only a few pounds. My hand reaches out to grab a piece of my husband. "If there is anything you need or if you have any questions, please feel free to give me a call. Again, I am just so sorry."

I nod absently at his sentiment, but I can't pull my

eyes away from the bag. This bag holds the last things my husband touched. If I had known he wouldn't be coming home tonight, I would have stopped him from flying out the door this morning. I would have grabbed him for another kiss, or hug, or just stared into his eyes. Instead, the last memory I have of my husband, Eric, was his trademark smirk as he walked out the door.

For the last time.

Blake shakes Frank's hand as Crystal drags me away from their whispered conversation. She pulls me into a separate room where she closes the door behind her.

"Listen, Hailey. I know you want to see him, I do. I know. But I'm going to be very honest with you. You won't recognize him." She stops talking as she takes a deep breath. "I promise you that if I thought seeing him would help you, I would bring you to him right now, but it's not Eric. It's not your husband."

I look into her eyes and see the pain in them. Is that how I look right now? Tortured? "This is a dream, right?" My eyes well with tears, and I have no chance of stopping them as they flow freely down my face. "This isn't happening to me. It's not him, right? It's just a terrible misunderstanding. That's the only way any of this would make any sense."

"I'm so sorry, honey. It's him. I wish I could take your pain away. I would do anything to take it away." She wraps me in her embrace, running her hands up and down my arms, the heat burning my arctic skin. My sobs start quietly, but before long, my wails are echoed down the hallway as I allow my eyes to close and let the darkness take control.

"I caught her before she hit her head," I faintly hear Crystal tell someone. I open my eyes as I'm lifted off the floor for the second time today. Blake carries me out of the hospital, my hand still clenching Eric's brown bag against my chest. I'm in a daze as Crystal opens the passenger side door, and Blake gently places me on the seat, pulling the seat belt across my body and clipping it into place.

The bright sun from earlier is now dull, and the birds no longer chirp. The only sign of life is the kids riding their bikes, laughing as they chase each other down the street. The streetlights flicker on as we turn down my street. We haven't said one word to each other the entire ride, and the radio has remained silent. Blake parks the car, but I don't make a move to get out. My arms are heavy, holding the brown bag like a lifeline. Suddenly, the car door opens, and Crystal, who I didn't even notice came with us, reaches over me to unclip my seat belt

"Let's get you inside," Blake says as I turn woodenly and get out of his truck.

I'm not prepared when I walk into our home and see Eric's jackets hanging by the door. The way his sweater from last night is just tossed on the couch, his morning coffee cup still sitting on the side table. Walking over, I grab the empty cup with just a drop left inside. "He just got home last night." I look up. "Maybe if he hadn't come back, he would still be here. Maybe…" I trail off in a whisper. Crystal and Blake share a glance. He moves to the kitchen, and she walks to me.

"Why don't I take you upstairs, and you can lie down for a bit?" Crystal asks. I nod and make my way to the stairs. I look back at the mug and brown bag I placed by his sweater on the couch.

"Don't touch his things," I tell them, looking over my shoulder. When I walk into our room, I take in the bed, still unmade from this morning. The sheets thrown over on my side. His work pants are tossed over the chair in the corner with his boots on the floor right next to them. His bathrobe tossed over the end of the bed. Picking it up, I wrap it, and his smell, around me. I fall on the mattress and close my eyes, hoping when I wake up, this will all just be a bad dream.

My eyes flicker open as I look around the dark room. I'm still in my bedroom. Our bedroom. My body feels stiff from sleeping on my side, and I'm still wrapped in Eric's robe. It's dark outside, but I know this wretched day isn't over.

"Is it real?" I ask the room, or better yet, I ask Crystal, who I know is beside me. She wouldn't leave me, just as she knows I wouldn't leave her if the roles were reversed. Since our mothers are sisters, and Crystal is only six months older than I am, we've been best friends since birth. No soul alive knows me better than she does.

"My chest hurts. My heart hurts." I whisper the last part, and I feel her scoot over and put her arms around my waist. The tears roll down my cheeks. "Did he suffer?" I ask. She'd know since she was there when they brought him in.

"No," she says quietly, her voice cracking as I hear her sniffle behind me. "He was already gone when they brought him in."

"Do you think he knew today was going to be his last day?" I ask as my eyes focus on a blinking star in the sky. "Do you think he knew? What am I supposed to do now?" Rolling over, I look into her eyes. She doesn't have the answers. No one does. I close my eyes, and once again, I let the pain take me. Take me to memories of when my life was happy, when my life was perfect.

I think about when I first met him. How opening a door to the local pizzeria changed my life. I wasn't even watching where I was going, and I smashed into his hard chest. His hands flew to my arms to make sure I didn't fall to the floor. "Sorry," I mumbled, looking up into chestnut-colored eyes.

His brown hair fell onto his forehead as he smirked at me. "Not a problem," he said as he dropped his hands. "I'm just glad I was here to help." I realized my palms were still on his chest.

"Um ..." I looked at my hands, then his face, smiling at him. "Thank you." I put my hair behind my ear. "If it wasn't for you, god knows where I would be." I

crossed my arms and laughed.

"I'm Eric." He reached out his hand as he intro-duced himself with a smirk that brought out his dimple.

"I'm Hailey."

"Do you want something to eat?" Crystal's voice breaks through my memory, bringing me back here. Where the pain is. My hand goes to my chest to rub away the pain or at least try. "You need to at least drink something." She gets up and walks out of the room, leaving me alone. I take a moment to look around our bedroom. I feel like a stranger in this room, like I shouldn't be allowed to touch anything. The picture of us on our wedding day taken only six months ago. I wish I could say I got my big fairy-tale wedding, but since Eric was a foster child, he had no family, no sib-lings, and his job required him to travel a lot. He nev-er really made friends, so he wanted a small wedding. "Just you and me," he said as he kissed me in the mid-dle of our backyard while we promised to love, honor, and cherish each other until death do us part. I was so in love with him I didn't care where we were married as long as we were together.

Tears pour down my face as I think of how my fam-ily crashed our small wedding. My brother, Blake, and his best friend brought over the meat while my parents came in with balloons and flowers. The small, intimate ceremony with just the two of us actually ended up be-ing thirty, but I wouldn't change it for the world.

"Your mom wants to make you something to eat

even if it's just toast," Crystal says as she walks back into the dark room with a glass of water in one hand and a coffee cup in the other.

"I'm not hungry," I whisper as I turn back around and smell his pillow. "He's really gone?" I ask her, looking at her, hoping it's just a mistake. A horrible mistake.

She wipes away a tear from her face as she walks toward me and takes a seat on the end of the bed. "We will get through this. I promise you." I just shake my head at her because there is no way to get over this. No way for the hurt to go away, the pain to dull, or for that emptiness to be full again.

"I don't think I will ever get over this." I close my eyes again, letting the now familiar darkness take me away. To the dreams of when Eric was here. When he smiled at me. Laughed with me. Kissed me until we were breathless.

When he loved me.

Chapter Two
Hailey

"You really need to get up," my mother, Joanne, says from beside me as she moves the hair away from my face. My eyes blink open, trying to adjust to the light from the side lamp by our bed. "I fixed your favorite dinner." She didn't need to tell me what it was because the aroma of fried chicken had made its way upstairs. Dinner? I slept through the night and the entire next day?

"Do you think he's here?" I ask her looking, trying to catch a glimpse of something, anything, telling me he's been here. "It hurts so much," I tell her, seeing the tears roll down her cheeks.

Eric was my husband, but he was like a son to my mother and even called her mom. From the first time they met, they formed a tight bond. The way she looked after him, and the way he took to her was a thing of beauty. They were so close. She could ask him anything about his past, and he never hesitated to give her the truth. He was always willing to help her with anything she needed. The way my family welcomed Eric with open arms made falling in love with him so easy. From cookouts at my mom's house to the fishing trips with my brother and father, it was like we'd always known him. Like he was always a part of our family. The only downside was his relentless traveling. Being the top mechanical engineer for Boeing had its up and downs. It meant we spent our first Christmas apart because he was stuck in Alaska. I never knew when he would be gone or when he would be back. But when Eric was home, he was with us one hundred percent. "I think I need to call his boss," I finally say as I look at her.

"Blake can do it for you." She leans down, kissing my forehead.

I shake my head. "That's my responsibility." I don't need to say anything else. Mom can tell I need to do this, so she just nods.

"Why don't you wash your face, come downstairs, and eat a bit? Then we can make the phone calls and worry about everything else." I sit up, my head spinning from all the sleep and tears. I climb out of bed and head to the bathroom. When I emerge, my mom takes my hand and guides me down the stairs.

Even though I bought this house the year before Eric and I were married, it had always been our home. Touches of Eric were everywhere. Frames capturing our happy times fill the walls. Pictures of just him, just me, but mostly, pictures of us together. Walking in the living room, I see the flowers he bought me every week just to say he loved me. In the kitchen, I see the coffee mugs he collected from his favorite football team, the Dallas Cowboys. Eric was everywhere I turned. Everywhere I looked.

Blake, my father, and Crystal sit at the table set for our dinner that my mother cooked, but the only thing my eyes focus on is that brown fucking bag on the counter. The last items my husband touched.

Walking to the counter, I grab the bag, feeling the rough, thick paper under my fingers. Everyone in the room stops moving, and it's so quiet; the only sound is my unrolling of the bag.

Opening the bag, I reach inside, my heart banging away in my chest. My fingers grab his watch first. I take out the black Invicta diving watchand and see that the face is cracked. The time is stuck at 12:11. The sobs rip through me as I close my eyes and hold the counter with one hand, bringing the watch to my nose to smell him. But it only smells of steel instead of the earthy smell I've come to associate with him.

I place the watch gently on the counter; reaching back inside, I pull out his wallet. The worn-out brown wallet that he always kept in his glove box because he hated to carry it in his back pocket. When I open it, pieces of glass fall on to the counter. I close it and place it next to the watch. My shaking hands reach back inside and pull out a black iPhone. I turn it in my hands, flipping it over, and confusion mars my face. "This isn't his." I turn to look at everyone. "His phone was white."

Crystal comes over. "Maybe it was put in there by mistake." She stands next to me as I press the middle button, and it shows me that the battery is dead. "Here, let me plug it in, and we can see who the phone belongs to." She grabs it from my hand, plugging it into the wall charger. I turn around and again reach into the bag. His white iPhone comes out, and when I press the middle button, a picture of us lights up the screen. Eric's sitting behind me on the steps of our porch. He had leaned down and kissed my neck, looking up just in time for the picture to snap. My finger rubs his face on the screen as I see his sweet smile and brown eyes. My eyes close, the pain and emptiness in my chest spreading through me. "We took this picture last week after he got home. He was gone for a month this time. It was the longest he'd ever been away." I look up at them. "How did this happen?" I ask as I look at each of them.

They don't have time to answer because the phone on the counter starts buzzing, the vibration moving it along the counter as we all look at it. The buzzing stops when I walk over to it and pick it up. The screen black again, so I press the home button. My husband's smile greets me once again, but it isn't his face that I stare at. It's the smile of the blonde who stands next to him as he has his arm around her and two children who stand in front of them. All four of them smiling for the camera.

The phone slips out of my hand, landing on the floor right at my feet. The picture looking up at us as the phone rings again. This time, the picture that comes up is that woman with the name *Baby*.

I look up to see my mother with her hand to her mouth and my father holding her shoulders. I bend down, picking the phone up as if it weights more than a hundred pounds, and press the green button to talk.

"Hello." My voice is shaky and low as I hear a child crying in the background. The woman's trying to soothe it, but stops as soon as she hears my voice.

"Hello." I hear a voice almost as soft as mine. "Who is this?" she asks as my hands start to shake, and I feel myself get lightheaded. My hand clutches my chest as I answer her the only way I know how. "This is Hailey."

"Who is Hailey?" I hear her ask, but I feel like I'm having an out-of-body experience. Like I'm watching this horrific scene play out from the outside. "Who are you?" I ask. Knowing the answer to those three words was about to change my world even more than it had in the past twenty-four hours.

"I'm his wife."

Three different words that take whatever may have been left of me. The phone again slips out of my hands, and my legs finally give out. My brother rushes to catch me as the phone hits the floor, the screen shattering. Crystal bends to pick it up and walks out of the room.

My head is spinning. My heart beating so fast it's likely I'm having a heart attack. I rub my hands up and down my chest as if somehow that will alleviate that permanent crack that has formed. It feels as if someone stuck a knife right between my ribs, and they may as well have. There is no way to get over a pain like this. It's less than a minute old, and even in my fucked up state, I know it's a forever kind of pain. I stare blankly into my brother's eyes as he yells my name over and over again. The blackness is back, coming to take me away. I try to keep my eyes open, but my lids are so heavy, so I stop fighting. Besides, when the darkness comes, nothing hurts.

In what seems to be a pattern, my brother carries me through the house and lays me on the couch. I listen to the chatter around me.

"What do you mean he's married? How could he be married when he and Hailey got married six months ago?" I hear my mother ask the question I'm sure I would ask if I could. If I could form a rational thought.

I try to force my eyes to open, but they feel so heavy. My arms do too. I just allow myself to surrender to the darkness. I don't know how long I stay locked away, but I feel someone sit down next to me. "I don't know the whole story," Crystal says softly. She picks up one of my hands and checks my pulse. "She told me they have been married for twelve years." The gasp from my mother startles me, and I'm finally able to flicker my eyes open.

"How long was I out for?" I ask as I sit up. Looking over at the clock on the wall, I see I have been passed out for over three hours.

They both stop talking and look at me. "Don't stop talking. I want to know. I *need* to know." My eyes implore Crystal to continue. My mother just nods and turns her head to yell for my brother. "I spoke to her a little bit till Blake took the phone from me. Blake!" she calls out. My older brother, my protector, walks into the room, carrying the black iPhone.

"Hey, sis," he says as he spots me sitting up, sliding the phone in his back pocket. "Tell me," I say, my voice louder than expected.

Blake looks at me and then looks away. "It's not a good time. You need to rest." He looks around for the others to support him. Lucky for me, my father shakes his head. "She needs to know, Blake."

"We all need to know," my mother says, walking to my father and wrapping her arms around his waist.

Blake sighs, wearing the resentment he has to be the one to tell us this all over his face. "Her name is Samantha. They live two towns over. They have been married for twelve years. She lives right next door to her in-laws. Eric's parents."

I start rapidly shaking my head. "Eric was in foster care. She's lying."

"No," Blake snaps, and my eyes fly to his. My brother *never* raises his voice to me. "His parents are alive and have been married for forty years. He has two brothers. He is the middle child." Blake pauses. "Are you sure you want to hear all this?"

My legs start to bounce up and down with nervous energy, "Just tell me, goddammit," I yell at him as Crystal comes over to sit next to me, grabbing my hand.

"Tell her Blake. She deserves to know." She looks

at me while addressing him.

Blake takes an audible breath. "They have two children. Daisy is eight years old. Liz is five years old. Last month, they found out she's pregnant again, but she miscarried shortly after. According to Samantha, they have been trying for the past year, but he got busy traveling, so it has been hard." He looks down as tears fill his eyes. I can tell whatever he's about to say just might be the final nail in my proverbial coffin. "His family is on their way to get his body," he finishes, his voice trailing off.

I shoot to my feet, this time yelling. "Get his body? What does that mean?"

"It means they are going to the hospital to get his body and take him home." He runs his hands through his hair.

I just stare blankly at my brother. "His body *is* home." I glance over at my father, who is a lawyer. "I mean, he lives here. We have paperwork." I make my way to the drawer where we keep the papers for our life insurance and also our marriage certificate.

"Honey ..." my dad starts.

"NO!" I yell.

I start pacing the room. "No." I shake my head. "He is my husband." I angrily brush the tears from my face. "We got married. We have a marriage certificate." I open the drawer, tossing the papers out as I look for the paper.

"Mcintyre isn't his last name. It's his middle name," my father informs me, stopping me as soon as my hand grabs the paper I'm looking for. My eyes read both our names. "It's null and void because well, honey, he is already legally married."

"No," I tell them almost shouting, "he told me he didn't want to use the name on his license because that was his adopted name and he wanted me to have his real name." I look at them and they all look down not making eye contact. "I want another lawyer," I inform him, narrowing my eyes at him. My father is the best family lawyer in town. Crystal gets up and walks toward me. I know she's coming to tell me more crap I don't want to hear, so I put my hands over my ears like any mature adult would do. "No! Don't you fucking say it. My husband just died. I have to plan a funeral, and you're telling me that I can't do that because he isn't my husband." I shake my head. "I don't believe you."

"Baby," my father says, that word sending shivers down my back after seeing it on Eric's "other" phone. "There is nothing you can do. If anything, they will say you were his mistress." His words are a slap in my face, freezing me in place. "Or the other woman. You have no claim to him."

"How can you say that to me?" My hands come down slowly from my ears. "I have all the claim in the world to him. He died here. Here in my fucking car. In my fucking town. He is mine." The sadness is gone, replaced by the anger pouring out of me.

"Hay—" Blake starts.

"NO!" I yell as I grab a picture of us from the side

table. We took it the day after Christmas when he finally made it back home. I hold the frame to my chest, squeezing it so hard, my fingers turn white. "I won't let them."

"Honey," my father says, "you have gone through so much in such a short time. How about you just rest, and we will figure it out in the morning? We will take a step back and see what needs to be done." At that moment, someone knocks on the door. Blake stands to walk to the door, and when he opens it, we all gasp.

"Eric?" I stammer out as I take in the man at my door. This stranger looks exactly like my husband.

"No. My name is Elliot," the man says as I walk to the door. He takes me in as I get closer and closer to him.

My eyes never leave his as I reach out to touch his face. "Eric," I whisper, not believing what I'm seeing.

He looks down as my hand falls from his face. "I'm Eric's older brother, Elliot. This is his younger brother, Ethan." He motions to the man standing beside him who I didn't even notice. "Um, sorry to barge in on you all, but ..." He looks down at his feet, putting his hands in his pockets before he looks back up. He takes a deep breath before finishing. "We are here for his things."

"His things?" I ask confused, looking from one face to the next.

"What things?" Blake comes to stand beside me. "Are you fucking kidding me right now?" he growls.

"Listen." Ethan puts his hands out as if he means no harm. "This is a difficult time for us all right now, but we need his wallet and hospital paperwork." He looks down at the floor again, unable to meet my eyes. "I don't know what my brother was doing or what he was thinking, but right now, our main concern is the two little girls he left behind. The two little girls who are without their father. And left with more questions than answers. That is our only concern right now."

"He said he was an orphan." I start telling them as my fingers hold the picture closer to my chest. "That he had no siblings. No parents. *Nothing*." I look at Elliot. So much like Eric, yet so different. "We got married six months ago." I look down as I feel the strength come over me. "Our entire life together is a lie. *Was* a lie. Everything I thought was real was, well, not." I shake my head and walk away from them to the kitchen. Grabbing the brown bag that held all his secrets and lies, I shove the watch and the wallet back inside with more force than necessary. Next, I drop in the phone he apparently used only for me. To continue his life of secrets and lies. But I don't care. I'm pissed. It's a lot easier to feel angry than to allow all the other emotions I'm feeling to bubble over the surface. I stomp back to the living room and start gathering everything that belongs to Eric. I grab his baseball hat, sweater, blanket, and the book he's been reading and toss it at the other brother, Ethan.

"That's all you're getting from me. This is all I will give you. You want something else? You're shit out of luck because I have nothing left to give you. Or you could sue me for it. That should be fun for everyone.

Sue the other woman for everything she has left of her dead fake husband." I toss my head back, laughing.

"Jesus. Can you imagine." I catch their eyes before looking at Crystal. "Lies," I spit out. I can't stop laughing. Or crying. I'm not even sure. "We were going to try for a baby." I put the palms of my hands on my knees. "He wanted to see me carrying his baby." I look back at his brothers, and I can't tell if they feel sorry for me or just think their brother conned a crazy woman. "Maybe he got me confused with the other wife. I mean, I'm not sure how these things go. I've never lived two lives before. But I could see how someone would get confused."

I look down at my wedding band and pull it off my finger. The same finger Eric slid the ring on only six months before. Reaching my hand out to Elliott, I whisper, "This was his also. Take it. I obviously don't need it anymore."

Elliott looks at Blake for help. My brother walks over to me, gently taking the gold band out of my hand and handing it to Eric's brother. "I think it's time for you to leave." They nod at us and mutter out a stilted, "Sorry." They walk out the front door, taking the pieces of Eric with them.

"I don't feel well." I look around at my family. "I think ..." I say right before I rush to the sink and dry heave.

"I think she needs to take something. To calm her down. To help her sleep," I hear my mother tell them.

"What she needs is to fucking forget that the lying

piece of shit ever fucking existed," Blake grumbles.

"Why?" I say softly and then shake my head. "WHY? TELL ME!" I yell out to Blake. "Why did you tell them where I lived? WHY WOULD YOU BRING THEM HERE TO MY DOOR?" I rush at him, shoving him back, or at least trying to. My brother is a solid brick wall and holds his ground. "Why! Why! Why?" I shout over and over and over again while I pound my fists on my brother's chest. I direct all the pain in my body into his chest, and the exertion leaves me crumpling down to the ground. Vaguely, I feel Blake's arms go around me again, cradling me against his body as he carries me upstairs to my bedroom. But I don't say anything. My body spent, my mind tired, and my soul empty.

Chapter Three

Hailey

I wake the next morning, my body aching, my eyes burning. I lie in my bed, my eyes blinking to take in the room

I stretch my legs in front of me, the smell of coffee making its way up to my room. "Who is down there?" I ask, knowing that Crystal is behind me.

"Your parents stayed the night and so did Blake," she whispers from beside me. I turn on my back now, looking up at the ceiling.

"My chest feels like someone is sitting on it." Rubbing the middle of my chest, I'm trying to get the ache to go away. I throw my legs off the bed and make my way down the stairs. The shades are closed all around the house, and the weariness fills the rooms all around us. My mother and father sit at the kitchen table with coffee in front of them.

My father's eyes tired and bleak; my mother's are still filled with tears especially when she sees me walk into the room. The front door opens when Blake comes in, a box of doughnuts in one hand and a bag holding McDonald's in the other. "I didn't know what you would feel like, so I got one of everything." He puts the bag in the middle of the table, but no one reaches for it.

When Crystal comes downstairs, she walks into the kitchen, going straight for the bag in the middle of the table. "You didn't get any hash browns?" she asks with a shrug, taking an egg biscuit out of the bag.

"What am I going to do?" I look around the room at everyone. "I don't even know when or where the funeral is?" I wipe the tears away. "I don't even know anything about him really."

"I can call his brother and ask him?" Blake says, pulling out a chair in the middle of the table. He is just about to reach for the bag when the doorbell rings.

The blood drains from my face, scared to face whoever is at the door. My mother looks at me, my brother getting up from the table to walk to the door. He unlocks the door and opens it, finding a man with glasses standing there.

"Can I help you?" he asks the man.

"Hailey Williams?" The man asks for me, and I walk to the door.

"That's me." I step in front of my brother, taking in the man with the khaki pants and the polo shirt.

"You've been served." He hands the papers to me. My hand reaches out to grab them as he turns and walks away, down the step to his gray Honda Civic.

"What on earth is this?" My father gets up and

comes to the door, taking the papers out of my hands and opening them. "You have to be fucking kidding me." He flips the pages over, looking up at me and then at my brother.

"What is it?" I ask, walking to him.

"You've been served a cease and desist letter as well as a restraining order against his wife and their children." My eyebrows pinch together as I look at the papers and see Eric's name. "You are not allowed to mention Eric, and if you do, they will sue you for slander."

"What the fuck," Blake yells. "They were in a relationship."

"According to the papers, they are also saying you have been stalking him and his family, and if you attend the funeral, you will be arrested for trespassing."

The sob rips out of me; my hand going to my chest, trying to rub the pain away. "I can't do this." The fight left in me gone.

"She has to be able to go to the funeral. She has to have closure," my mother says from besides me on the floor.

"Joannie, we can't do that," my father says. "I'm going to call the office and see what can be done, but"—he shakes his head, looking down at the paper—"it doesn't look good."

"What did I do?" I ask the room, all eyes on me. "What did I ever do to them?"

"You did nothing to them," my brother says. "Not one fucking thing." I just nod at him, then slowly get up and walk back up the stairs to my room. But instead, I go to the spare room, not wanting to lie on our bed without him. I look at the white ceiling while I listen to the sound my father asking questions on the phone. At the same time, Blake threatens to go down there and beat the shit out of his brothers, and Crystal tells him she is going to start the car.

When my father comes upstairs, he finds me still looking up at the ceiling. Walking into the room, he sits by my side. I move my head to the side, looking at the defeated look in his eyes. "There isn't anything we can do."

"I know," I tell him, softly reaching out to hold his hand.

"I think we should go to the funeral anyway and say fuck them." He squeezes my hand.

"No, I won't put you guys through that." I blink as tears fall out of my eyes and onto the pillow. "I won't give them the satisfaction to do that to me." The tears don't stop. "I won't let them have that hold on me." He nods his head while my eyes give into the burning, my lids closing.

One Month Later

"This is fucking horse shit," I hear Crystal yell from somewhere in the house. Her footsteps pounding up the steps get closer and closer to where I am. She storms

Into the room that is dark and pushes the curtains open, letting sunlight come blaring in.

"What the fuck, Crys?" I groan out as I try to swallow past the cotton balls stuck in the back of my throat. I cover my head with the covers. My head's spinning and throbbing.

The covers get ripped off me. "Get your ass up," she says as I moan and try to grab the pillow beside me, but the only thing I touch is the empty bottle of wine I came to bed with.

"GET UP!" She now yells at me.

"Jesus." I squint one eye open. "What the hell is your problem?" I ask, folding myself out of bed. Dragging my ass to the bathroom, I'm hoping she'll be gone when I get back to my bed. I wash my face, rinsing my cotton mouth out with water. Opening the medicine cabinet, I grab the Advil and shake three into my hand, leaning down to drink water from the sink faucet. I close the cabinet, avoiding the mirror. I don't need to look into the mirror to see that I look horrible. Walking back into my room, I find Crystal has stripped my bed sheets off, and wine bottles fill the trash can beside the bed. How long has that been full? "What are you doing?" I ask her, leaning against the door so my head will stop spinning.

"I'm doing this tough love bullshit that I should have done last week, but Blake said to give you one more week." She grabs the sheets in her hands as she walks down the hallway, bypassing the room I refuse to step into. I've been sleeping in the guest room for a month now, or maybe longer. What date is it? I turn my head, watching her toss the sheets into the wash. "Get up and get dressed. We are going out for food. Real food, not a bag of chips, or a frozen pizza, or ice cream. A whole meal."

I close my eyes as my head finally stops spinning or at least dulling. "I don't want to go out," I whine as I approach the bed and sit on it. "Outside bad, inside good." I try to joke with her, but she just glares at me.

"You don't have a choice in the matter; either you come on your own, or I bring out the big guns." She walks into the room with her hands on her hips. "What is it going to be?" she asks again.

"You wouldn't dare bring out the big guns." I point at her as she pulls out her phone and taps a couple of things. "You have three seconds to decide, or I'm calling Nanny, and she is going to be the one to get your ass up." I look at her in shock—bringing Nanny in is a low blow, even for her. Nanny is our eighty-three-year-old grandmother who has seen enough of her own heartache to last a lifetime. She was married at twenty-two and widowed at thirty-two with three children and a debt bigger than Mount Everest. But she put on her big girl panties and thrived. Making her bigger than before. She never did remarry, and now she is the event coordinator for seniors living. She has a busier social calendar than Crystal and I combined.

"That is not fair," I tell her as Nanny's voice suddenly fills the quiet house.

"Knock, knock, knock," she says from downstairs,

and our wide eyes fly to each other. We scramble around the room, hiding the wine bottles under the bed. I rip the dirty shirt over my head, smelling myself as I do and almost gagging. I open a drawer and see a Tweety shirt I haven't worn since I was sixteen years old. Trying to put it on my head, I get it stuck with only one arm in it. "Where are you girls?" We hear her walking downstairs, and I huff. Crystal runs to me, trying to help me put my other arm in.

"Why the fuck do you still have this shirt?" she whispers as she yells, "Upstairs, Nanny." She grunts as we try to get the shirt past my boobs, but it stays stuck under my armpits.

I can't move anymore with the shirt stuck under my armpits. "Fuck, try rolling it down," I tell her while I work on one side, and she tries the other.

"This is almost like Cinderella's stepsister with the big clown feet trying squeeze into a dainty shoe," Crystal says as she gets it almost over one boob before it just rolls back up.

"What in heavens are you two doing?" Nanny says from the doorway. Her perfectly coiffed white hair rests on the shoulders of her all-white outfit paired with a deep purple jacket and matching necklace and brace-lets. "And what is that smell?" she says as she tries to discern where the smell could be coming from.

"That smell is Hailey," Crystal points out as she walks away from me to give Nanny a hug. "She smells like horses." Turning to me and smirking, she says, "Want to go out to lunch, Nanny?"

"Um. Only if that one showers." She points at me, and I roll my eyes.

I smile at them. "That's perfect because I don't want to go out anyway. You two have fun." I shoo them away with my hand.

"Hailey, you haven't left the house since …" Nanny starts saying and then slowly stops talking. "It's not healthy. I mean, honey, you look like …" She throws her hands up and then continues, "You look a mess. Your eyes are sunken in, and you have bags under them big enough for one of Marie Antoinette's dresses."

I fold my arms over my chest. "Yeah, well. I'm okay at home by myself."

"You aren't the only one who lost a husband," Nanny says to me, catching me off guard

"Actually, I didn't lose a husband, according to every single letter that I have gotten after Eric's death. I'm basically nothing to him. So I lost a friend," I tell them angrily as a tear escapes my eye, and I brush it off, angry that I'm again wasting my energy on him. Every letter I've gotten from the time he died just reinforced that I was nothing to him. From the life insurance policy that got denied to the bank letter that froze our joint account. It has been one clusterfuck after another.

"Good. Now that we have that settled, get yourself in that shower and let's go get something to eat." She doesn't give me a chance to answer. Instead, she turns around and walks to the stairs. "Oh and carry all those wine bottles shoved under the bed out to the recycle bin." She doesn't bother turning around to see our mouths open and then close again.

"I'll get the bottles; you hit the shower. I would wash twice if I were you. And shave the pits because it isn't appealing," Crystal says as she gets down on her hands and knees to grab the bottles. When I get to the bathroom, I cut myself out of the shirt with a pair of scissors. I finally look up and see the shell of a woman I once was. My blue eyes are bleak, empty, dull. My long blond hair oily and stringy.

"Fuck you, Eric," I say to the empty room while I shower and wash and shave. By the time I finish, I feel almost semi human. I try on a pair of jeans, but when they almost fall off, I opt for a black tank top with a cream and black maxi skirt.

With my black flip-flops on my feet, I walk downstairs, braiding my hair to the side. I find them in the kitchen with the shades open, finally letting the sun in. A stack of mail on the counter is falling over, since I only open the ones I think are important. Soft music plays from the radio on the counter. Nanny is scrubbing the food off the dirty dishes piled in the sink while Crystal opens a couple of windows to let the spring air in. Birds chirp in the background—fucking birds chirping—and the sound takes me back to that day. I blink my eyes to stop the memoires from seeping in. "Okay I'm ready," I tell them when they both look up at me. "Where are we going?"

"I made a reservation at the Garden Inn," Nanny says, and I throw my head back and groan. The Garden Inn is the local hangout where everyone goes to have a home-cooked meal. It's the last place you want to go when you are hiding from everyone and everything.

"Can—" I don't have time to finish before Nanny wipes her hands on the tea towel and turns to smile at me.

"I'll drive," she says, not giving me a chance to back out. I look around the kitchen and see Eric in everything. Seashells that we collected on our honeymoon from the beach sit on the windowsill. Magnets on the fridge of places he'd left me for. Lies. I walk to the fridge, take them all down, toss them into the trash, and then walk out of the room.

Nanny and Crystal don't say anything as they follow me outside to my overgrown lawn. The plants Eric and I potted last month sit on the porch dried up and dead. "I need to cut the grass," I mumble, walking down the steps to Nanny's car with my head down the whole time. Opening the back door, I get in and finally realize I forgot my purse. I open the door to get out when Crystal shoves my purse at me. "Thank you," I mumble as I open it and take my shades out and put them on. I buckle my seat belt as I look out the window and see that the world hasn't stopped. Life keeps moving. People are still getting up and going to work, kids are still in school, and life goes on, yet I'm the one still stuck in place.

After we arrive and park, I get out, trying to blend in, but I feel all eyes on me. I look down at my feet. "This is a bad idea," I say quietly as Nanny gets on one side of me and Crystal gets on the other side. My protectors.

"Nonsense," Nanny says as we walk up the steps. Opening the door, she steps in, and when the bell rings above the door, all talking stops. I'm about to turn around when I hear Nanny. "Oh Edith, good, you're here. I called about a table for three. I hope it's okay that we are early," she says loudly, not caring that people are looking and probably judging me. I should just wear the big red letter A on my chest.

"Sure thing, Sheila," she says as she walks. Edith is going to give us a table in the back, but Nanny stops walking in the middle of the restaurant. "We will take this table right here." Nanny motions to the empty table in the middle of the fucking room.

"Seriously?" I say under my breath as Nanny pulls out a chair.

"This is perfect," she says. I sit with my back toward the door but face Nanny with Crystal in the middle of us. I grab the menu Edith hands to me with a smile and a thank you.

"Um, do you guys want to start with something to drink?" she asks as she takes out her pad.

"I'll have a vodka on the rocks."

I take my glasses off as Nanny laughs. "She's kidding. We'll all have some sweet tea." Edith nods at us and walks away. I look around and find people trying to avoid eye contact with me. "This was such a bad idea."

Nanny closes her menu in front of her. "Why? Why do you think this is a bad idea?"

She waits for me to answer. "Because people are staring at me and whispering. It's like I'm a circus animal let out of the cage," I tell them both and then look at my menu, but all the words are all over the place. I'm not even looking at them.

"What are you afraid of?" Nanny starts and then doesn't wait for me to give her an answer. Instead, she answers for me. "Are you afraid people are going to see you smile? Are you afraid people are going to judge you? Are you afraid someone is going to tell someone else that you were out and living?" I shake my head. "Newsflash, you are already at your rock bottom, so how much more can you go down?"

"Wow." I laugh bitterly, grabbing my glass of water that Edith had just filled. "Don't sugarcoat anything, Nanny."

"I won't," she says. "I've been where you were. Actually, it was worse. He left me three kids to raise by myself."

"Really?" I ask. "At least your husband was your husband."

"Well, sometimes, I wish he wasn't. He left me with three beautiful kids and more debt than humanly possible to get out of. But guess what I did?" She smiles and waves at someone who just walked in. "You have nothing to hide from. You didn't fuck up, that dickhead did." She looks at Crystal. "I never liked him."

I roll my eyes. "You lie. You loved Eric. Fuck, everyone liked Eric. I used to get the 'Where is Eric?' before you asked how I was." I finally smile. I think it's my first smile in a month.

"Honey, he is gone and not coming back. So you have two choices. One, you wallow, which I have to say you've been doing quite well, or two, you dust yourself off and live again."

"I chose three," Crystal says. "Purge him from your system."

"She can't have sex with someone now; she isn't in the right head space," Nanny says. "I mean, she would probably cry in the middle of it."

"Are you two done?" I ask, relieved to find everyone back to normal and no one listening to us. No one is pointing anymore, but I see a couple of people look over, smile sadly, and then turn around and continue their meal or conversation. The meal is long or, at least, it feels long. I ordered soup but pick fries off Crystal's plate. When Nanny drives us back home, we wave goodbye to her as the walk inside the house feels stale, stiff.

Sitting on the couch, I feel the memories come floating back. "I hate this house," I say as I grab the remote and turn on the television.

Crystal hangs with me until she has to go to work, and then I sit on the couch all night flipping through the channels. Night turns to morning as my eyes never tire or close, but my mind spins.

I finally get up sometime after dawn to walk upstairs to the bathroom and then make my way to the spare room. I look at the bed and realize it's not made. The sheets are still in the wash. So I turn around and look at the closed door.

The door I shut a month ago; the door I swore never to open again. I walk toward it slowly, the floor creaking under my soft footsteps. My hand reaches out to grab the handle, feeling the cold metal under my warm hand. Turning the handle, I push the door open slowly, the hinges squeaking when I finally push it all the way open.

The stale air has specks of dust floating in the sunlight streaming in the side windows. The bed sheets lay crumpled from when I first got home on that fateful day. The pictures on the side tables have a light layer of dust on them. I still smell him; it's faint but it's still there. I walk in, treading lightly, almost as if I'm the stranger in the house. As if I don't belong here. As if this isn't my room.

I walk toward the closet and open it, seeing his dress shirts hanging there, waiting to be worn, but I know they will never see the light of day.

Taking one out, I bring it to my face, hoping to smell him or feel him, but instead, I smell soap. I place it back then go to his side table, opening the first drawer.

My hand traces the Kindle that sits on top of everything else.

When I spot a flashlight, I take it out and turn the light on. A rubber band from the music festival we went to last month sits in the corner, and another watch he needed a battery for is tossed to the side.

I spot the condoms, right beside everything, and laugh awkwardly. "Well, we know why he didn't want to have kids right away. Asshole," I say out loud, hoping he's here, hoping he can hear me. I slam the drawer closed and march downstairs.

Grabbing a garbage bag from under the sink, I storm back upstairs, this time whipping open the closet door. Yanking his shirts off the hangers, I stuff them in the bag. Some hangers fly to the floor while others just dangle on the rod empty. Empty like this house. After filling up the bag with his clothes from the closet, I walk over to his chest and open the drawers to find his t-shirts all folded perfectly. I pick them up and toss them into the bag. Drawer after drawer till the bag is almost full. I still have a couple of drawers left when I hear the doorbell. Looking over at the clock beside the bed, I see it's almost ten thirty. I open the door and come face to face with a huge bouquet of red roses in a beautiful crystal vase. "Um, I have a delivery for Hailey," the man says as he takes in my rumpled attire.

"That's me," I tell him as he hands me the bouquet and walks back to his yellow van.

After I close the door, I walk into the kitchen and place the roses on the table then pull the card out. Finding the front of the white envelope blank, I turn it over and flip up the flap, taking the card out.

Thank you for opening that door one year ago and changing my life.
Forever Yours,
Eric

The sob escapes me no matter how much I try to fight it. My hand covers my mouth, and my legs get wobbly. My hand holds the table as the card falls to the floor, floating left and right before it lands right by my foot. My hand shoots out, tossing the vase to the floor and shattering it into a million pieces.

Chapter Four
Hailey

I sit in that chair watching the tiny crystal pieces glitter in the sunlight, afraid to move in case I slice open my bare feet. The door opens, and my brother, Blake, comes in. "Hey," he says from the door as he walks into the kitchen. Taking in the shattered vase and the roses in a heap on the middle of the floor, he hears the crunching of glass under his boots. "What the fuck is this?" he asks as he spots the card. Bending down, he picks it up and reads it. "Cocksucker had everyone fooled." With a shake of his head, he walks to get a broom and dustpan then cleans up the floor. As he's pulling the vacuum out, another knock on the door has us both looking up.

"Knock, knock, knock," Nanny says as she walks in.

"What the fuck is this? Grand central station?" I try to get up but then sit back down.

She comes in with papers in her hands. "Oh good,

you're up." She takes in the roses tossed in the garbage can with the shattered glass on top of it, but the look from Blake tells her not to ask. "So yesterday after lunch, I was thinking you need to get away. I think …" She holds her hand up when I open my mouth to speak. "Hear me out. You aren't comfortable here; you sat here yesterday hoping to fall through the floor. Don't deny it," she says. Blake finally finishes cleaning up and sits down in front of me. "I got home and called my oldest friend, Delores. Remember her? She came down a couple of summers ago." She opens the papers she is holding. "Anyway, she owns some houses that she rents out down in the Carolinas right on the water. And she has one available for as long as you want it." She pushes the paper to me, and I take in the picture of the house. The only thing my eyes go to is the swing hanging on the front porch. The house looks cute and quaint. I flip through the pictures, taking in the backyard, and see another swing, but then I see the ocean, the calmness of it.

"She just can't leave," Blake says as Nanny looks over at him.

"And why not?" He doesn't answer because Nanny doesn't give him a chance to. "She has nothing here. Nothing. Yes, she has her family, but she needs to find herself. Staying here in this museum she calls a home isn't helping anyone. Besides, she can work from home. All she needs is her computer, and she is good to go."

"Yes." The sound comes out in a soft whisper.

"Yes." I look up as Nanny smiles and Blake scratches his head.

"Good, but I will tell you that no one has been in that house for over four years, so it's dusty and you'll have to clean it yourself."

"Okay." My fingers move over the swing in the picture. The weight of everything lifting off my shoulders a bit.

"I want to have a yard sale." I look at my brother. "I want to sell everything. I want nothing."

I look at Nanny. "Will you help me?"

She puts her hand on mine. "I'll make the posters today." She gets up and walks to the door. "I guess this is like that song 'Cleaning out the Closet.' Remember, Blake? You used to sing it each day in the mirror wearing your white t-shirt and your jeans hanging low under your ass." She laughs. "Until I told you that inmates wear their pants like that to have …" She cups her mouth with her hands and whispers, "Butt sex."

I snort as Blake throws his head back. "Oh, good god," he says as Nanny slams the door on her way out. "You sure you want to go there and be all by yourself?" he asks me, looking at me for an answer.

I don't have to answer because Crystal comes in. "Hey, you guys," she says, tossing her purse on the couch and coming in to start the coffee. "Whatcha looking at?" she asks as she picks up a picture of the house. "This is so pretty."

Blake fills her in. "That is where Hailey is going to, as Nanny says, 'find herself.'" He uses his fingers to make air quotes.

She doesn't say anything, so I ask, "Okay, who wants to help me with this garage sale?" I look around. "I think I want to sell the house." They look at each other and then at me, both nodding. "I know I had this house way before Eric ever lived here, but I can't live here, not after." I don't bother talking. Instead, I nod and get up, going to the fridge.

No one said anything, but we did end up cooking breakfast, and Blake called someone he went to school with about listing the house. By the time night came, the walls that had felt like they were closing in on me stayed the same.

I lie awake most of the night, my mind working a mile a minute as I think about the next step in my life. The next chapter of my book.

My mother and father come over the next day as soon as the real estate agent hung her sign. I stand there on the porch in jeans and a sweater, my bare feet cold on the cement porch. "Your grandmother was not kidding when she said you are making changes," my father says as he carries in grocery bags. "We brought you some food." I watch them both walk in with their hands full.

"I also told your aunt Ginette to come and help organise things," my mother says of her sister and Crystal's mother. I just nod as I look down at the card from the real estate agent. She said it should sell quickly. I look around, seeing my next-door neighbor outside. She was always very friendly, but this time, she just smiles and raises her hand to wave.

I do the same as I now sit and take in what I thought would be the house where I would raise my kids, where I would mark their first everything. Instead, I think of all the lies it holds.

I shake my head as a tear comes out, and I realize it's been eighteen hours since I last cried. It might not be much to anyone else, but to me, it's a step in the right direction. The front door opens behind me, and my mother comes outside to sit next to me. She puts her arm around my shoulder, and I lay my head on her shoulder. "I really hate him, Mom," I say as she squeezes my arm. "I hate what he did, but most of all, I hate that I will never know why. Why the fuck did he marry me if he was already married? Why create this life with me when he already had it all? Why? That is all I want from him."

"Oh sweetie, I don't think you would have ever gotten those answers. They say everything happens for a reason, and I have no idea what this reason is, but it has to be for something bigger, something better. I honestly believe that, and you have to also." I don't say anything else. I don't want to tell her that it's all a lie. There is no reason this happened and no good that could come from this. Nothing.

We stay out till the sun sets, only getting up and going in when Dad's cooked his famous lasagna and my aunt comes over. "Hey there." She puts her purse down on the couch. "It smells so good in here, Henry," she tells my father as she opens the oven door to smell the lasagna he made. She comes to hug me, and I shed tears. She must know because she doesn't let me go. "It's going to be fine, little girl." She has always called me little girl, since I was the baby.

"I think I'm going to take a shower before we eat," I say and quietly excuse myself to go upstairs. I take a shower and get out right as Crystal knocks.

"It's me," she says, and I tell her to come in.

"We never will get closure," I tell her as she closes the door and blinks at me, not sure what to say. "I mean, we didn't have a funeral. We didn't have"—I throw up my hands—"well, anything. It was just here today, gone tomorrow. Oh and your whole life was a lie." I shrug.

"It wasn't all a lie," she says softly. "He had to love you to try to do the whole *Sister Wives* with you. Even without you knowing you were the second wife." She tries to smile. "You didn't even pressure him to marry you. That was all his idea."

"I know," I say as I put my bra on. "I never once said you need to pay for the milk because this cow isn't free." I mimic my Nanny's words. "He was the one who wanted to get married right away."

"You don't know if he was happy; I mean, maybe the other woman …" she starts, and I put my hand up.

"Samantha, her name is Samantha," I say as I lotion my legs.

"Okay, fine, Samantha. You don't know whether he was happy."

"I don't even want to discuss him, and nothing you

could say would ever lead me to understand why he did what he did," I tell her as I put on a sundress and tie my hair on top of my head. "Nothing."

She holds up her hands. "Fine, fine, fine. Do you want to maybe have a celebration of his life?" I glare at her, and she puts up her hands again. "Fine. Okay, okay." She drops the subject as we make our way downstairs, and I see that almost my whole family is here with the arrival of my other cousins Lydia, Victoria, and Peter. They just smile at me as they take a plate and go to the dining table. Extra chairs have been added so everyone can squeeze in.

I just take in the love and support of my family as Nanny arrives with cake. "Oh good, I'm not late," she says as she air kisses me and brings the cake to the kitchen.

"What the hell is going on?" I lean in and whisper to Crystal who watches everyone moving around my house with me as she shrugs.

"It's a celebration of YOU," Nanny says when she walks into the room. "To show you how much we love you." She smiles as she grabs the plate Ginette hands her. "Thank you, dear." I shake my head as tears start to form. "Hey, none of that. Besides, we need all the help we can get to move this stuff outside for tomorrow."

I smile as I sit down, and it feels like old times. I'm in this bubble of love, and I know that no matter what happens from here on out, it's going to be okay. I mean, how much worse can it get?

Chapter Five
Hailey

"I can't believe we sold everything," I say to Blake as I bring my bag to my car and put it in the front seat. He follows, carrying out my two suitcases. I look back at the house with the lights on inside, the sun peeking out from the horizon. The bright red sold sign sticking up. It took three days for a cash offer to come in, and here we are, seven days later as I load my car and make my way down to my escape house. That is what we are calling it.

I donated Eric's clothes to the homeless shelter and then sold off everything else he had in the house. His tools were the only thing I kept, and I gave them to Blake—under protest, since he didn't want them. I may have lost a husband, but he lost the closest thing he ever had to a brother.

He shuts the trunk once he places the luggage inside, and I lean in to hug him around his waist. "What am I going to do without you?" I ask him as tears start to form in my eyes.

He smiles down at me. "You know I can be there in eight, maybe seven hours. Just call and I'll be there." I nod my head as I hear a car stop behind us.

I turn to see Crystal get out of a strange car. "You came to say goodbye," I say, wiping the tears from my eyes.

"Pfft," she blows out. "As if I would let you leave without me," she says as she opens her trunk and pulls out two large suitcases.

"What is this?" I ask her as Blake grabs them and puts them in the back seat.

"This is me and you taking on the world," she says, smiling as she wipes tears from her own eyes.

"You can't come with me; you have a job here," I tell her as Blake laughs, and I turn and glare at him.

"No, I had a job here. Now, I have a job there." I look at them in question, so Crystal continues, "I left my job, but good news, I got one in town. It's a family practice. No gunshot victims and no stabbings, so it will be a walk in the park."

"You're coming with me?" I ask her, shocked and happy at the same time.

"Of course, I'm coming with you," she says as if it's the craziest thing in the world.

"But," I say stuttering, "but we had a goodbye dinner last night."

"Well, it was a free meal. How could we not?" she says as she grabs another bag from her car. "So what do you say? Should we start our new adventure?"

I smile, looking down at my feet. "I have to lock up the house," I say as I walk up the steps. "Um, if it's okay, I'd like to do this on my own." I don't wait for them to answer as I walk inside the empty house. I'm taken back to when the house was filled with laughter, when it was filled with love, when it was filled with promises. I walk to the kitchen, thinking of the first time I cooked for him, and then he made me breakfast the next morning. I flip the lights off, heading upstairs.

The bedroom door is open with the blow-up mattress that I slept on gone. The room where we spent most of our time, the room where we told each other our dreams and our hopes ... gone. I close my eyes, trying to hear his voice one last time, but nothing is there. Nothing but emptiness and silence. I shut the light off before I grab the door and close it for the final time. "Coward," I whisper, hoping Eric hears me. I turn around and wipe a tear from my face. Walking down the stairs one last time, I turn off the final light and look at the darkness.

I lock the door, making my way to the car with Blake leaning on the back trunk next to Crystal. "Here is the key." I hand him the key to the house. "The real estate agent will stop by the firehouse at three p.m. to pick it up." Blake is a firefighter, and he's on shift this week. He grabs me around the neck and pulls me to his chest where I sob out the pain I'd pushed aside the past two weeks; the pain I thought was gone but was only lingering.

His arms around me comfort me till I'm spent, and

my eyes are sore and heavy. "Good thing I'm coming. Who else would drive?" Crystal says as she gets on her tippy toes and kisses Blake's cheek. "I'll call you when we get there," she says as she walks to the driver's side door and gets in, leaving me standing with Blake.

"How did you do it?" I ask him, thinking of his first true love, Frankie. Francesca came into his life when he was fifteen. In high school, both of them joined the debate team. It was a friendship that blossomed into love until her cancer claimed her five years later, leaving Blake broken. He has not dated since that day. It's as if he's stuck in that place.

"Don't do what I did. Don't shut yourself off from the world. Live," he says. "Promise me you'll live." I smile as I place my hands over his two hands on my cheeks. "You have to listen to me. I'm older," he says, causing me to laugh out loud.

"Yeah, yeah," I say to him as his hands leave my face, and I nod. "Promise me the same." He nods at me, putting his hands in his back pocket as his green eyes still stay shaded and protected.

"Get out of here," he says as he walks back to his truck. "See you next month for sure." I nod at him, climbing in the passenger side.

Crystal starts the car and slides on her sunglasses. "Isn't this just like Thelma and Louise?" she asks, and I laugh to myself.

"Can we do it without the whole driving off the cliff or shooting Brad Pitt?" I ask her as she pulls away from the curb.

"I say we still shoot Brad Pitt but don't die either. I mean, imagine if one of us survived without the other." She shakes her head as I lean my head on the cold window. Basking in the sun, I see a bird soaring in a circle in the sky. "I'd come back and haunt you. Just saying." I laugh, taking my eyes off the bird to look at her. When I turn back to see where the bird went, it's gone.

I watch the trees as we make it on the highway on our way out of town, the sign telling us they hope to see us again. "I start work next Monday," I tell her as I take my phone out and see that my emails have gotten over ten thousand. Before all this happened, I was a highly sought-after web designer. You had a business that needed a website, you contacted me.

"So in four days," she says. "That's perfect. I start Monday also," she informs me. "I spoke with them on the phone, and their practice is family run. A father and son. I spoke with the father, but I haven't met the son yet. From what I gathered on line, they are the best in the region. It should be fun."

After four hours of driving, we stop to get gas and use the bathroom. I grab some food for us, and we get back on the road for the rest of the journey. Having the both of the windows down allows the country air to settle in with us. My hand reaches outside, and I let the wind blow it back before pushing my hand through it. The mountains in the distance get closer as we make our way there and finally turn off the interstate at our exit. With trees lining the street on both sides, we follow the directions, turning once to go down Main

Street. I laugh; it seems every city or town has a Main Street.

Passing over a little bridge, we watch the creek on both sides, the water flowing down. Once we get off the bridge, I see every single shop has the American flag hanging outside. As we slowly roll down the street, I look at my side of the street and the sidewalk consisting of tiny red blocks. The D'Amore pizza place has a red and white sign with green around it. I look inside and see someone tossing a pizza in the air behind the counter in the middle.

Right next door to the pizza place is Sweet Pixie Cuts. I try to look inside, but all I see is white. A small cast-iron table sits in front with two pink chairs.

Next is Grandma Susie's Kitchen, and looking inside, all I see is red and white. A couple of people are sitting on the stools right at the front. A waitress carrying food with both hands. A billboard in front displays today's specials written in pink chalk.

A big green awning with white writing hangs in front of the next shop. Tina's Treasure Thrift Shop has racks of clothing lining the front two windows. A big cardboard BOGO sign in black hangs in the window. People walk down the street and wave to everyone. "I think everyone knows everyone," I comment. Taking off my sunglasses, I realize more shops are across the street. "We should take a walk tomorrow night," I say as Crystal turns left in the front of the pharmacy, which just has the mortar and pestle on it. We pass the courthouse, or at least that's what I think it is because courthouse is written in the middle of it. I see a tavern on Crystal's side but don't catch the name as she turns left again to head into what looks like a development of new houses.

We continue down and pass a cul-de-sac with two houses on the street. I see a little girl riding her pink bike with her father chasing after her as she laughs and tries to get away. We turn down a gravel road, and I take in the lush trees on both sides as we get to the house. The white house looks deserted and nothing like the pictures.

"What the fuck?" I say as Crystal puts the car in park right in front of the house. I look up and see that one of the black shutters is falling loose from the window on the second floor. I open my door and climb out of the car, meeting Crystal in the front to take in our new home.

"That picture lied," she says as she grabs her phone out of her pocket and calls Nanny. "I know you're not answering because you know why I'm calling," she says into the phone and then hangs up, turning to me. "Maybe it's just the outside." She digs through my purse for the key. "Let's go inside and see how bad it is." We walk up the front steps and find one whole step missing.

I shake my head as we make it to the door, turning and seeing that swing that called my name. The chains that hold the swing are rusted and covered in spider webs. The wicker seat is so dirty, and the pink rug that was under it is blown half over. "Okay, so we need to do a couple of projects," I say as she puts the key in the door and turns the lock. "Well, at least we aren't locked out," I say as she pushes open the door and steps inside.

The huge living room is empty. The fireplace has a board nailed over it with a single white chair in the middle of the room facing it. The gray floor has seen better days. I turn the lights on, but they just flicker. We walk in to see the kitchen to our left with a wooden island in the middle and all the cabinets white and lifeless. The brown wooden butcher block counters provide the only color in the room. The white porcelain farmhouse sink faces the window looking out to the front. The windows have no shades. The white gas stove with black burners has seen better days as has the fridge. Crystal walks to it and opens it and groans at the smell. "We need to buy a new fridge and stove," she says as I look around, thinking with the right couch and table, this place can be perfect.

I follow her down a short hallway where we find a simple bathroom on our left. The black and white flower tiles on the floor dress it up a bit, and a see-through curtain covers the window. I open the door on the right and find a huge master bedroom. Three windows face the water in the distance. Noticing again the white walls, I walk in and open the door to the bathroom. "Why is everything so white?" I say as the floor creaks under my feet. The ceiling in the bedroom was a dark wood, but someone painted over it. As is evident from the brown fan that sits dormant with spider webs hanging from it. Heading out the door in the corner of the room, I take in the covered porch and the other swing that drew me to this house, but I don't look at it. Instead, I listen to the sound of the rumble of the ocean and the waves crashing on the shore. Looking out, all I see is the darkness of the night. "This is so cool," I say as I glance at the swing. This one has some padding on it and gold chains holding it up.

"Good. I'm not taking this room," Crystal says as she walks back inside the house and tries to find light switches that work. I follow her as she heads to the living room and walks up the stairs, where we find two more bedrooms with a huge bathroom with a sunken tube. After we walk to the back of the house, she picks her room, and I decide to make the third bedroom my office. "Fuck. Where the hell are we going to sleep tonight?" she asks as we walk back downstairs, and I turn in a circle.

"We are going to sleep here," I tell her as her phone rings. She answers right away.

"Nan, you have so much explaining to do," she starts off, and I turn, looking back at the fireplace, and sit in the chair, almost falling since one of the legs are broken. "It's empty," she says. "Like so empty I don't even think racoons would live here." She continues as she walks toward the back of the house. "Yeah, yeah. Well, you'd better call your friend and tell her that we need the super of someone to come and clean this shit up." She presses the button to end the call. "I don't think there is a super." She looks at me. "We need to hit up a Walmart or a Target," she says as she brings up her maps. "What the fuck? The closest Walmart is an hour and four minutes away."

I nod my head, going outside and grabbing our bags to carry inside. "An adventure," I tell her as she glares at me. "Come on, we can stock up on all the stuff at Walmart, and tomorrow we can go shopping for a couch and stuff." I smile at her, and she follows me outside. We get back in the car, and she drives us one hour and four minutes away to the closet Walmart. I look out the window, never once shedding a tear.

Chapter Six
Hailey

My eyes blink open as the sun hits my face. I try to stretch my body, but it's stiff, and my joints groan out in defiance when I roll over and hit the floor. That is what we get when you choose a blow-up mattress that sits on the floor. After huffing and puffing about our 'dire' situation, Crystal and I hit up Walmart. Let me just say we are so much more prepared now than we were last night when we arrived.

We had three carts overflowing with everything from cleaning supplies, to towels, to bed sheets, to a coffee machine, toaster, food, and our blow-up mattress. But we didn't stop there. Nope, not us and our adventure.

Before we even made it into Walmart, we shopped at Country Sam's Shop For Less Furniture and Supplies next door. Well, I have to say I was like a kid in a candy store. While Crystal made sure she had a king-size bed and matching armoire, I went on the hunt for our couch. And what a couch it was. We decided on two couches with big fluffy pillows; to me, it felt like sitting on a cloud. I was so excited that I bought even more throw pillows while Crystal sat on the couch the whole time. We added a white table with six chairs, which was a bit big since we didn't know anyone here, but I know my family will visit. I picked the most feminine bed in the store. Fuck, if they'd had a pink one, I would have chosen that one. But I went with a white one instead. I couldn't wait for them to deliver it Saturday.

I go to the bathroom and wash my face, then come out to the kitchen and start the coffee. I see that it is just after seven a.m. I slept a whole three hours. Once the coffee is made, I grab one of the throw blankets we bought and make my way outside.

When we arrived yesterday, I saw stairs off to the right that I knew led down to the ocean. Grabbing my flip-flops, I make my way outside, down my backyard steps, and walk over the short grass to the wooden stairs.

I stand on the top step and breathe in the salty air. Watching the water crash down on the shore as my hair flies in my face from one side, I smile at the calmness and peace that I feel at that moment.

Coming out in a tank top and cotton pants wasn't my smartest move, so I wrap the blanket around my shoulders as I walk down the steps. My feet sink in the sand as soon as I step off the last step onto the sand. As

I walk down the grass-lined path, I come to a wooden fence but half has fallen down. I get closer to the water, the sound louder as more and more waves crash.

I sit down, glad I brought the big blanket, and watch the waves come at me, careful to sit far enough back so I remain dry. The coffee in my hand gets cold faster than I can drink it. It's almost like drinking iced coffee by the time I place the empty cup beside me. My thoughts take over, and I make mental lists of everything that needs to be done. I'm watching the waves so intently I don't even see the little girl running along the water until I hear her giggles when the water touches her rubber boots.

Watching the carefree little girl makes me smile. I look back and see a golden lab run in the water and then back toward her. She stops running and puts her hand on the dog's back. "Mila." I hear a man's voice yell out. "Mila. You're too far," he says again as the dog sits by her side. She waits for the man to come closer. He is wearing pants and a sweater with a baseball cap on, covering his eyes.

When he gets closer, she turns and runs ahead, but when her head turns, she sees me. Her dog jumps in front of her, trying to catch her attention, but she runs over straight to me. "Are you lost?" she asks as her dog barks at me, and my head snaps back.

I don't have time to answer because her father comes running and grabs the dog by the collar. "Sorry," he says. "Flounder, stay." He orders the dog to sit next to him while he pants, and his tail moves on the sand.

"I'm sorry, he really is a good dog," he says as he pets his head and then squats down in front of his girl. "Mila, what did I tell you about talking to strange people?"

The little girl's little curls fly into her face, a strand going into her mouth, and as she reaches up to move it away, her raincoat falls off one shoulder. "Poppa, she lost." She points back at me as the father now looks up at me, and for the first time, I see his face. His blue eyes cloudy and almost a dark blue, just like the ocean I'm looking at. His lips full as his cheeks are covered with stubble.

"I'm not lost," I tell him and the little girl. "I just moved into that house," I say as I point back to the white house.

The minute I mention the house, his demeanor changes, and his back goes straight. He stands up, grabbing his little girl's hand. "She isn't lost," he says as he pulls her away from me with the dog following them. I sit there in shock at what just happened. The man bends down and picks up the little girl, and she hugs his neck with one hand and waves bye to me with a little smile. My hand comes out of the blanket and my fingers bend as I wave back to her. I watch them walk back down the beach, the dog running in and out of the water, until they are no more than a speck in the distance.

I sit out there for a while, watching the water as it slowly inches closer and closer when I hear footsteps behind me. "Dude, my whole body is stiffer than a ninety-year-old on Viagra," Crystal says as she sits next to me, and the visual causes me to snort. "So Ms. This Adventure is so Cool, Delores called, and she is coming over in about thirty minutes to see us. Apparently, Nanny filled her in." I don't answer her. Instead, she stops talking as she looks at the ocean, and we get lost in our thoughts until she gets up and holds out her hand to me. "Let's go." I grab her hand to help me up, and we walk back inside.

The toast pops up as soon as we hear a knock on the door. I look at Crystal, who gets up and walks over to the door to open it. "Hi," she says to an older lady with gray hair that looks almost silver. "Please come in." She moves away from the door as I lean against the now clean counter, bringing my coffee cup to my lips.

"Oh, dear." The woman looks around as she takes in the room. "I had no idea," she says as she looks at me. "You must be Hailey." She comes into the room and spots the fridge. "What in the heavens?"

"I take it you didn't know how bad the condition was?" I ask her, and she shakes her head.

"This house belonged to my grandson and his then wife. Before she took off, that is," she says. I just nod at her and sip my coffee.

"Would you like a coffee?" I offer her, and she smiles at me. "I mean, you have to stand and drink it." I smile back at her, silently high fiving my humor.

"I would love one," she says, "Can I look around?"

"Please feel free," I tell her as Crystal starts making her a coffee. "The couches and beds are due to be delivered on Saturday," I tell her, and she looks at me with her eyebrows pinched together.

"We don't get anything delivered on the weekends. Besides, this house needs a new paint job before anything comes in."

"Um, well, I start work on Monday, and there is no way I can continue sleeping on a blow-up mattress. So they'd better be here on Saturday with my bed or else." I look at Crystal, waiting for her to finish her sentence, but she doesn't, and then Delores walks out of the room.

"Or else what?" I ask her as she points at me.

"Don't fucking start. I will, I don't know, poison their fucking cattle. Or"—she throws up her hands— "tip over a cow. Don't fuck with me and my sleep."

I fold my lips trying not to laugh as she glares at me and Delores comes back downstairs.

"Okay, girls, pack up your stuff. You will stay with me until your furniture is delivered." She shakes her head. "I'm so, so sorry that you had to sleep here last night. This is the only property Jensen blocks off from being rented, but I had no idea," she trails off, "that it was this fucking disgusting." She looks at us. "Excuse my language."

Crystal comes to stand next to me and lean on the same counter as Delores takes a pad out of her purse and writes her address on it. "This is my address. It's on the other side of the development." She writes something else. "This is the code for the gate. Luckily, I have no cattle for you to tip over or poison." She winks at Crystal. "Now, this is the address," she says as she tears another paper off, "to the construction house. I want a list of everything that has to be done. Right down to all the sockets. I will make sure everything is finished this weekend." She hands me the address. "Now, I hear you had a shitty month." She grabs her cup of coffee.

"A shitty month is a good word for it," I tell her as I put my cup down. "I mean, I've never found out that my husband was already married with a family before, so my vocabulary might not be up to par." I laugh. "But shitty about sums it up."

"Love works in mysterious ways. Sometimes, it comes when we aren't looking for it or least expecting it." She shrugs her shoulders. "I mean, I don't even know how I would have handled your situation," she says.

Crystal laughs. "She didn't really handle it." I glare at Crystal. "I mean, she wallowed, but she didn't handle it."

"How would you have handled it?" I ask her, folding my arms across my chest.

"Me?" She points at herself. "I would have probably burned down the house and then told his parents what a fucking douchebag their son was. After I stole his body and kicked the shit out of him."

I gasp as Delores laughs. "See, a reason it didn't happen to her." She tilts her head to one side and smiles as she finishes her coffee. "Now, I have to run. The club is having a spring mingles meeting." She grabs her purse. "Pack your things and come on over."

We nod at her as she walks out and gets into her huge Cadillac truck. I look over at my cousin. "You so wouldn't have stolen his body. You lie." She shrugs her shoulders as she walks toward the stairs.

"We will never know. Now, let's make that list so we can get a nice hot shower." Taking a notepad out of my work stuff, we go room by room, and by the time we finish, I've filled two pages, front and back, with a bit on the third page. After I dress in tights and a sweater, we make our way to the construction office. We pass Main Street again, turning left on Walker street. We continue to the end of the street and see the medical clinic right in front of us. The construction house is on one side and the firehouse on the other side. When we park in the parking lot and get out, Crystal says, "I'm going to go into the clinic, if that is okay." I nod at her and make my way over to Walker Construction.

Walking up the steps to the big log house, I open the door. When the bell over the door rings, the blond receptionist looks up. She smiles at me. "Hi there, how may I help you?" The phone rings, and she holds up her finger. "Walker Construction, how may I help you?" I turn around and take in the room; a fireplace sits in the middle of the room with the company logo on the top. "I will have him call you back as soon as I see him, Delores," she says as she hangs up the phone. "I'm so sorry. Now, what can I do to help you?"

"I'm looking for Jensen," I tell her. Her smile fades

a touch, and her eyes go from smiling to a flicker of something else I can't put my finger on. "I'm renting one of his properties," I tell her, and her smile returns.

"Of course," she says as she picks up the phone and presses a button. "I have someone here for Walker, but I think she needs to see you," she says. She nods her head and hangs up the phone. "Brody will be right out, if you want to have a seat." I smile at her as I walk over to one of the chairs and have a seat, but a second later, a big, burly man comes through the back doorway. He is about six-foot-four, his hair past his shoulders, and I take in his huge chest. He looks like a huge lumberjack. His plaid shirt rolled up his arms, he ducks to come out. "Hey there." He smiles at me as he reaches his hand out. "I'm Brody."

"I reach out my hand to shake his, and he nearly shakes my arm out of my socket. "I'm Hailey," I say, pulling my arm back. "I'm the one renting the house on Pine Street." And as soon as I say the address, his eyes go big.

"If you would follow me." He turns and walks back down the hallway. I take in the offices on each side, and after we walk all the way to the end, he turns right into his office. "Please sit down." He motions to the two chairs in front of his big wooden desk. A deer head hangs on the wall right in front of me. "So you are the one?" he asks as I sit down.

"I'm the one." I raise my eyebrows, smiling, not sure what is going on. "Um," I say, reaching into my purse. "We made a list of things that need to be done in the house." I unfold the papers and hand them to him just as the door on the left opens. I turn my head to see the man from this morning.

He looks at me and then looks at Brody. "We don't have time to do anything with that house." His voice comes out harsh, and I watch as Brody glares at him.

"Well, Delores told me to come by and give it to Jensen, and he would deal with it. So perhaps if someone got him, then maybe we can settle this," I say as I lick my lips, my mouth a little dry as my hands start to shake.

"I'm Jensen, but you can call me Walker," the man says. "No one calls me that except Grams." He comes in and snatches the list from my hands and looks it over. "No way in fuck we are doing any of this. You should just load your car up and go back home. You know, to your house that isn't here." My back goes up straight, and I stand as Brody follows suit.

"I don't know who pissed in your cornflakes this morning, or if you're just always this kind of, well, asshole, but I have a lease. A lease that is a binding contract." I swallow. I don't know where I get the courage, but I advance on him and snatch the list right out of his hands. "So if you aren't going to abide by the lease, and I have to live in deplorable conditions, then this is something that my lawyer may need." I turn back and look at Brody. "I'm sorry I wasted your time. I'll tell Delores to contact my attorney." I shrug my shoulders as Brody looks at Jensen and then back at me.

"Give me the list and I will send the guys over first thing tomorrow. It will be done by Sunday. I guarantee it even if we have to pitch in," he says, and I nod at him.

"Thank you for your help, Brody." I turn to walk out of the room but stop first. "And this is my home," I tell them and then walk out. Tears start to form, but they aren't sad tears this time. This time, they are angry tears. I storm out of the office as the receptionist thanks me for coming, but I'm about to flip her off as I slam the door and make it to the car. "Fuck you," I say to the empty car as I close my eyes and wait for Crystal to come back to the car.

Chapter Seven
Jensen

I wait until I hear footsteps go out the front door and then the door slam before I hang my head. My own hands digging into my hips. "Dude, what the fuck was that? I thought you were going to eat her head," Brody, my cousin and business partner, says as I look over at him. I shake my head.

"I met her this morning on the beach," I tell him as I close the door to make sure Kimberley doesn't hear any of this. "Mila and I were walking down the beach like we do every morning, and there she was, wrapped up in a blanket. Mila went to her first, and I thought she was lost. Fuck, she looks lost." I sit down in the chair that the woman was in.

Brody finally sits down. "I don't know about you, but the last thing that woman looked like was lost. She looked like she was going through something, but not lost." He folds his hands in front of him. "I told you someone was going to be staying in your house."

I cross my ankle on top of my knee. "I thought you were bullshitting like you always do."

"Not bullshitting you this time. She signed a one-year lease. Actually, Grams was the one who had her sign it. She goes way back with Hailey's grandmother," he says as I roll her name through my head.

"I want her out of that house," I tell him, getting up and going to the door. "Give her another fucking house. I don't care, but I don't want her in my house. Not now, not ever."

"Not your call to make," he says, leaning back in his chair. "She rented it, so that means she wants that one. Suck it up. Besides, it's been five years. How much longer are you going to hold on to the past?" he asks me, and I don't answer him. "Either way, this list needs to be done by Sunday, so you'd better fucking pray I don't call you in to help." He smirks at me, and I walk back into my office and slam the door. The frames on the wall shake as I look out the window and think back.

I walked up the steps of the house we had just finished building, carrying roses in my hand. Glancing at the swing where we'd sat last night, I smiled, remembering how it finished with me inside her. My Julia.

We met in junior high, and I fell head over heels in love with her. The moment she walked into class with her brown hair blowing in the wind, I knew she was the one. I stopped talking and made my way to her. "I'm Walker," I told her, and she blinked her eyes and looked down, only to look back up again and smile at me. From that day on, we were inseparable. Her family had moved to town when her father took a job as fore- man, working for my father. As the weeks turned into years, we were stuck to each other. There wasn't a time when I wasn't without her, so it was only normal for me to propose to her the day I turned eighteen. Surround- ed by our friends and family, we finally tied the knot the day after graduation. I was heading off to college, and she was following me. She wanted to be a nurse, but one year into the program, she decided to take a year off. So I continued with school, and she was a stay-at- home wife. Luckily, we didn't have to worry about rent since we were staying in one of my parents' homes.

When I finally graduated from business school, my father handed me the keys to the business. Two months later, he had a heart attack while eating breakfast. The hours were long and hard in the beginning. I had to make my stamp on it, but I had Brody by my side. Bro- dy was my cousin, and I brought him in as a partner the day after the company became mine. Then I hired my best friend, Scott, to be foreman for the jobs, since Julia's father had passed away.

It took me two years to get the company where I wanted it. Dad had a staff of twenty; I worked my ass off. My staff of fifty guys was all over the town, and we were doing business in the next town over. Walker Construction was never better, so I built us a home, surprising her the same day she told me she was preg- nant. I had everything I could ever want. On our fifth wedding anniversary, she completed my life by giving me Mila two months before I turned twenty-three. I had everything I ever wanted.

Julia sent me a message, telling me she dropped Mila off at my mother's house and would be waiting for me at home. I wore a smile the whole day. Since Scott had an emergency, I had to finish the job.

Tucking the roses into my hands, I opened the door to our perfect white house. "Honey, I'm home," I said out loud, taking in the rocking chair by the couch with Mila's toy basket next to it. I walked down the hall our bedroom and found it empty. I ran upstairs to see if maybe she was soaking in the tub, but she wasn't there. I took my phone out and called her, but her phone went straight to voicemail. I walked to the back deck to check if maybe she had fallen asleep on the other swing I installed on the back porch. Walking back inside, I set the roses on the table, and when I looked around, I spotted a letter on the fireplace. Right beside the picture of us on Mila's christening day.

I walked toward the letter as my palms sweat. I picked up the envelope with Julia's handwriting on the front. I turned it over, opened the flap, and pulled out the white letter.

Dear Walker,

I don't know how to start this letter, or even have the words to explain everything.

I want to start by saying that I'm so, so sorry.

I don't know how it happened or even when, but my life has been incomplete. I thought it was just me. I thought

I was just going through the motions, but nothing I did could fulfill this void I had. A void I didn't even know I had. Until Scott.

I'm in love with him. I guess there is no easy way to say this except to come right out and say it . I've been in love with him for over a year. I swear to you I never meant to hurt you. I never meant for this to happen, but it just did. I thought it would change as soon as I gave birth to Mila, but I felt nothing. It was just another anchor to keep me rooted in a town I now hated.

We just got the results back, and Mila is yours, so we won't be taking her. But I won't be coming back. I can't live a lie anymore.

I want to be his wife. I want to be the mother of his children.

We will be leaving this morning, and I will send the divorce papers as soon as we get settled. I don't want anything except for you to let me go.

Please, please forgive me and know that I really did love you.

Julia.

I looked at the other paper in there, proving with 99.97% probability that I was Mila's father.

My knees gave out, and as I fell to the floor, the letter in my hand was like a knife stabbing me through the heart. I looked down at the fucking letter and let out a roar. I got up on my feet and tossed everything on the fireplace mantel to the floor, including the picture of my sweet little Mila. Two-month-old Mila.

I put my face in my hands and sobbed out the pain, the pain from learning my wife just left me for my best friend. I was so stupid, so blind, and didn't even see it. The knock on the door shocked me as the door was pushed in and Brody walked in, taking in the disaster surrounding me.

"What the fuck is going on?" he asked. I just shook my head as he leaned down, picked up the letter, and read it. "Motherfucker," he said as he walked to the kitchen and took out the bottle of scotch I kept. He grabbed two glasses, and we finished it; or better yet, I finished it and fell into a stupor.

"Walker." I hear Kimberley's voice coming through the speakerphone, bringing me out of my memories. "Your grandmother just called again, and she said she is going to be here in thirty minutes if you don't call her back."

"Thank you," I tell her as I grab my keys off my desk and storm out. Getting into my truck, I head to my grandmother's house. She went too far this time. I pull up to the big ranch-style house my grandfather built with his bare hands. It's where my father grew up. It's where I licked my wounds after Julia fucked me over.

I don't bother ringing the bell and just walk in. "Where are you?" I shout out. "Meddling woman," I say under my breath as I walk into the living room. Looking in the kitchen, I see fresh blueberry muffins on the counter. I grab one and take a bite before walking outside where I hear her laughter. Storming around the wall, I stop in my tracks when I see Hailey. She is here, in my grandmother's house, sitting down having ... fuck if I know, with another blonde at the table. Grams looks up at me with a smile. "Oh good, you're here." I stand there, my feet stuck to the floor, and the blueberry muffin like glue in my mouth as the other two women look at me. Hailey glares at me.

"I need to talk to you," I say, pointing at my grandmother. My feet finally work, and I walk to the table. I'm about to say other things when I hear the door open and my daughter, Mila, appears.

"Poppa, you came to the tea party?" she says, running into the backyard as my mother follows her. I smile at her as she leaps into my arms and kisses my lips. No matter what Julia did to me, she gave me Mila. "Nana said GG is having a tea party." Her eyes go wide as she wiggles down from my arms and my mother makes it to my side. Nana is what Mila calls my mom, and since Grams wanted to be the hip great-grandmother, she chose GG.

"I didn't know you were joining us?" She comes closer to me, and I kiss her cheek.

I look over and see Mila sitting on Grams's lap, looking over at Hailey. "You aren't lost." She shakes her head, reaching for a cookie. "Poppa," she yells out, "she's not lost." She smiles at me, and I nod at her.

"Um, Grams, can I have a word with you?" I say out loud now as my mother looks at me. "It will just take a minute."

"Nothing to discuss, Jensen. Fix the house."

I clench my teeth together so hard I think I might actually break them. "That's my house, and I want her out," I say. Hailey looks at me with hatred ... pure hatred.

I'm not the bad guy here. "So you two need to pack up your shit and get out of my house."

"Poppa, shit's a bad word. Right, GG?" She looks up at my grandmother while she licks some chocolate off her fingers.

"They signed a lease." My grandmother looks at me. "A lease that is a binding contract."

"Oh, dear." I hear my mother next to me. "This isn't going to end well for anyone," she says under her breath. "Mila, come and wash your hands so we can start the tea party." Mila throws her cookie on the table as she claps her hand in glee. Getting off Grams, she skips over to my mother, takes her hand, and goes inside. I wait for the door to close before I turn back around.

"I guess we are going to see you in court because there is no way in fucking hell I'm renting out that house."

"My father is a lawyer," Hailey says finally as the other one just grabs her hand. "A good one. Technically, my name on the lease means I can come and go as I please. Unless you file eviction papers."

"Listen, I don't know what game you're playing"—I finally glare at her—"or if you came to lick your wounds because your husband didn't want you." I regret the words the minute I say them when Grams and the other woman gasp. Hailey's eyes fill with tears, and she gets up slowly.

As I watch one tear fall on her hand, she says, "If you'll excuse me, I think I need to lie down." She walks past me, and I watch her walk inside, her shoulders hunched over as she hangs her head.

"Asshole," I hear and turn back to the table as the other woman points at me. "Excuse me, Delores, I suddenly feel sick." She throws her napkin down as she walks away. I turn back and see Grams glaring at me.

"You think she wants to sit in your shell of a house while you wait for your wife to come back? Newsflash, Jensen, her husband just died," she says, and my stomach roils as I look back inside and see Mila talking to her as Hailey stoops down in front of her. "Except he wasn't her husband," she whispers, and I whip my head back.

"What the fuck are you saying?" I ask her, fearing the worst, but the minute she says the words, I know it's way worse than I thought. "He was married to someone else. So the life she was living was all a lie. So not only did her husband die, but she found out he was also someone else's husband first, leaving her alone and with questions he will never be able to answer." She gets up and comes to me. "So I offered her a place where she could try to live again. That house is yours, but that land is mine," she points out. "Fix it." She doesn't give me a chance to answer; instead, she walks into the house, and all I hear is laughing as I watch Hailey throw her head back with Mila in front of her giggling.

"What the fuck is going on?" I say to myself and the universe. While I wait for an answer, all I get is a text from Brody.

Tomorrow, the white house. I bought the paint.

I don't bother to answer, while I walk out of the backyard to the front. Instead, I pick up the phone and make some calls. Even if I have to muck and clean out the town sewer system, someone else will be taking my place.

When I look back inside the house and don't see anyone walking outside from the backyard, I look up at the house and my eyes land on the room in the corner. The room where I pulled myself together for my daughter, the room where I dealt with her colic, and the room that made me realize I could get through this. I see the curtains move as I look down and get in my car. Driving away, I never once looking back.

Chapter Eight
Hailey

"I can't believe you guys did all this in twenty-four hours," I say as I look around the house, which has a new paint job and working lights. I look over at Brody who stands there with his big arms crossed over his chest and his legs spread apart. "Even the outside looks brand new."

"I'm glad we could make it right," he says as I hear footsteps upstairs. "They are just finishing up the final touches. Miguel should be done in about five minutes, and then we will be out of your hair."

I walk into the kitchen, taking in the new stainless steel appliances, and open the fridge to find it fully stocked. "You guys didn't have to stock the fridge," I say. Crystal walks in with her mouth hanging open in shock.

"Holy shit," she says as she takes in the room. "You guys did all this in twenty-four hours?" she asks as she goes upstairs to her room. I hear her yelling, "Holy shit," and I look over at Brody who smiles. I hear her coming back downstairs. "You see what happens when you threaten to poison cattle?" she says, putting her arms out the side of her. "Boom. Mic drop." Her outstretched fist opens.

Miguel comes downstairs, nodding at Brody as he makes his way outside with his tool box. "See you tomorrow, boss," he says, turning to nod at us also. He walks out the new door as the new screen door slams shut behind him.

"Look at these appliances," Crystal says, opening the fridge and seeing it fully stocked. She grabs a bottle of beer and hands it to Brody, who takes it from her with a nod. She pulls out another two, one for each of us, and twists the tops off. "To the adventure finally beginning." We click the bottles then we bring them to our lips. I look out the window and see a big white truck backing up. "What is that?" she asks. Pushing off from the counter, she goes to the door, and I follow her. I see four SUVs pulling up alongside the white truck.

The only ones I recognize are Delores and Heidi, who introduced herself as Jensen's mother when we had the tea party. Delores gets out of her truck, and I see another tiny woman with bleached blond hair get out of her own SUV. She smiles at us and waves as she walks up the steps. "Hey," she says, her voice coming out soft. "Look at this house, it's almost brand new." She admires the swing that has been either painted or washed down.

"Hey, gorgeous." We hear Brody from behind us

move us to the side and grab the woman by her waist, lifting her up. "Give me some sugar," he says. The blonde just smiles at him and sighs, leaning in to kiss him. He puts her down as he drapes his hand around her shoulder, and she wraps her arms around his waist, her head reaching the middle of his chest. "Ladies, this is my wife, Darla." He looks down, smiling again as we both say hello at the same time.

Delores walks up the steps, dressed in jeans and a white dress shirt rolled up at the wrists. "Okay, enough of that lovey-dovey; we have a job here," she says as she takes off her sunglasses and smiles at us. "Now this," she says as she takes in the room once she walks into the house, "this is what I'm talking about." She walks to the kitchen and turns on the water, then goes to the fridge and opens it, nodding in approval that it is stocked. She turns on every burner on the gas stove until they all light up. She turns them off, then makes her way around the whole house, testing everything from the light switches to the sockets to make sure everything is in working order. "Okay, boys, let's get it done," she yells, and Crystal and I just stand there shell-shocked as three men jump out of the truck and move to the back and open it up.

I take in the back and see that it is filled to the brim. "What is all that?" I ask, looking around. Heidi just smiles at me as she approaches.

"This is everything you guys ordered." She points at the truck and tears escape me. "And stuff we also picked out as a thank you for not suing us." She comes to hug me. How did such a wonderful woman make the biggest jerk face on earth?

"So while the big, strong men bring in the stuff, us womenfolk will put it away," Delores says as she starts giving out orders. Brody meets the three other men by the truck.

"Ladies," he yells out, and we all turn around, "this is my best friend, Doug." He points at the biggest guy there. If I thought Brody was big, this guy is almost double his size. Doug just nods at us as Brody continues the introductions. "This is Kingston," he says of the middle one who is almost the same build at he is, and then he points at the last guy standing there with a blue baseball cap, black beard, and brown eyes. "Now this one is Gabe." He looks at Crystal. "And her boss." He points as I see Crystal's throat swallow down.

His hands go to his hips. "Can we finish this today, please? I have a shit load of stuff to do this afternoon." His voice comes out a little harsh as he jumps into the back of the truck and hands down a box.

"Holy shit," I whisper to Crystal. "Your boss is fucking hot." I look around, making sure no one heard us as I see Delores and Heidi open the cabinets and start placing plates inside.

"Why is he so angry?" Crystal asks in a soft voice, and I shrug my shoulders, but Darla adds in her opinion.

"There is not enough tequila in the world for me to get through that story," she says and then goes back to the kitchen as we watch two men bring in a loveseat.

For the next four hours, our little quiet home comes together. "Where are the car keys?" I ask Crystal, looking through her purse and then finally finding them. "I'm going to go get the boys pizza," I tell them, and they all cheer. Well, almost all. Gabe just glares.

I park in the back of D'Amore and walk to the front. The aroma of tomatoes hits me right away when I walk in. I look at the front counter and the man behind it pounding away at the dough in front of him. Another man adds wood to the big brick oven behind him. "Can I help you?" asks the lady standing at the hostess stand on the left.

"Yes." I smile as I walk over. "I'd like to order five pizzas," I say, counting off to make sure it's enough in my head. She hands me the menu so I can look at the different options except there are only three—cheese, pepperoni and cheese, and meat lovers. "Well, this is a hard choice. I'll take one cheese, two pepperoni, and two meat lovers." She smiles at me, then yells the order across the room, startling me.

"It will be about ten minutes. You can have a seat here." She points at the two chairs beside her. "Or you can sit at the bar in the back." She motions to the small rounded bar in the back corner of the restaurant. Wine glasses hang from the racks above the bar as the guy works quickly to keep up with the orders that come in. The restaurant is almost full. Where most restaurants have individual tables, D'Amore only has long tables with stools, and you sit where you want. Bags of flour line the walls as well as boxes of what look like tomatoes stacked halfway up the wall. I'm looking around when I see Mila stand on a stool and wave at me, calling my name. "Hailey." Pizza sauce all around her mouth. I smile at the little girl, then she looks down at her father and he turns his head to look at me. I wave to the little girl and then turn my head to look outside, forcing myself not to see if she got off the stool. I feel someone poke my leg, and I turn to see the little girl in question. I squat down in front of her. "Well, hello there, Princess Mila," I say to her as she smiles and giggles at the nickname I gave her. "You came out of your castle?"

"Yes." She nods. "Poppa just picked me up, and we get pizza when he picks me up at Grandma Norma's house," she informs me as her father now approaches. "Ready to go?" he asks Mila, not even giving me a glance. Mila looks up. "Can we go walk on the beach and find shells?" she asks her father, who just nods. She grabs her father's hand as I hear the man behind the counter call my name. "Have fun, Princess Mila." I tap her nose with my finger as I stand and go to grab the boxes.

The young man behind the counter smiles at me. His white baseball cap on backward makes his green eyes pop. The white t-shirt he is wearing is smeared with tomato sauce. The apron he has on just as dirty. "You're new?" he asks, and I nod. "I'm Luigi."

"Nice to meet you, Luigi. I'm Hailey." I introduce myself as I reach out and grab the five boxes of pizza, not expecting them to be so heavy. Who knew. "Wow.

That's heavy." I laugh as he reaches back to grab them from me.

"I'll help you carry them to your car." He is about to turn around, stopping only when he hears a gruff voice.

"I got it." I turn to see Jensen reaching past me to grab the boxes. "Mila, hold on to my leg, okay?" He looks down, giving his daughter the instruction, and then waits until she nods.

"It really isn't necessary. I can carry them; I was just surprised they were so heavy," I say to them, but Jensen is already outside. "Thank you so much, Luigi." I walk to the back and find him standing next to my car, waiting for me to unlock the doors. I take the key from my pocket and unlock the door. He opens the trunk and places them inside, then closes it. Grabbing Mila's hand, he walks away. "Thank you," I say, but he doesn't turn back around. Instead, he opens his truck door and buckles Mila in, then turns to get in and takes off, leaving me standing in the middle of the parking lot. "Asshole."

I shake my head as I get into my car and make my way back home, popping the trunk open and carrying the pizza inside. I walk in, taking in the room, and smile to myself.

The loveseats are perfect, the added throw pillows completing the look. A cream-colored quilt hangs over the back of the loveseat. The wooden box side tables hold two lamps I didn't buy, and there is a white coffee table in the middle with a wooden tray in the center containing the remotes and several candles.

A picture-perfect room with the now working fireplace and a television hanging just above it.

I walk to the antique white dining room table, which I knew would be perfect, and place the pizza on it. Heidi comes into the room from my bedroom. "I might never leave," I tell her, and she throws her head back and laughs.

"Food," Brody yells from behind me, and everyone gathers in the living room from wherever they were in the house. I look around and see Gabe and Crystal missing. "Where are the other two?" I ask as I grab a piece of pizza, folding it and taking a bite, the sweetness of the sauce hitting my tongue first. "This is so good."

"The other two are upstairs having a standoff," Delores says as she grabs a piece of pizza. "Apparently, there is a correct way to have the bed against the wall. One said straight, and the other wants it at an angle."

"Um," I say as Gabe comes storming downstairs. Walking straight out of the house, the screen door slamming behind him, he gets in Darla's car and leaves. We all watch as Crystal comes down the stairs wearing a smile.

She doesn't say anything. Instead, she grabs a piece of pizza, groaning, "This is the best thing I've ever eaten."

"What did you do to Gabe?" Darla asks from her husband's lap.

"I didn't say anything," she says, "He was ranting and raving and apparently me not saying anything pushed him over the edge. He fired me. I laughed at him." She laughs as she takes another bite of her pizza. "Then I took the phone out and called his father and quit." She shrugs her shoulders.

"You quit?" I shriek out while the other people in the room just laugh.

"Well, I tried, but Nathan, Gabe's father, didn't accept it and called his son." She shrugs. "I have no idea what was said. I mean, I saw the vein in his forehead start throbbing. Then I asked him if he needed medical attention because he looked pale."

Brody throws his head back and lets out a big belly laugh while Delores looks down and snickers. "Then he stormed out of here."

"This is going to be fun," Brody says, and Darla cuddles in his arms, laying her head on his shoulder. "Okay," he says, kissing Darla's head, "we are almost done. Let's get the last things out." Darla gets off his lap so he can head out to the truck with the other two guys and finish unloading.

Heidi cleans up as I walk to the back where my bedroom is, stopping at the entrance. "This isn't what I ordered," I tell Darla as I walk inside, my feet landing on a huge shaggy brown rug in the middle of the room. The king-size bed sits in the middle of the room between two windows. An wooden off-white bedframe holds the mattress, and the champagne-colored duvet covering it looks like a plush cotton ball. The side tables bring a bit of style with mirrored glass tops. A small plant decorates one of the side tables, and a big clock hangs on the wall next to one of the windows. A cream-covered bench sits at the foot of the bed with a plush cover. "It's a dream."

"I'm happy to hear you say that." I hear Delores say from behind me as she leans on the doorframe. "You need somewhere that is your sanctuary, and I want this to be it," she says as I wrap my arms around my waist, the tears coming now.

"It's not what you went through; it's what you do after it that defines you," she says, and I nod my head. "The boys just finished bringing in the last of it. We are going to let you two get settled."

"Thank you," I say to her as she looks at me. "Thank you for making me finally feel at home; it's been a while." She turns and walks away. I make it outside to the glass-enclosed porch, sitting in the wooden swing that someone sanded down, repainted, and added new cushions to, and look out the window. Seeing Mila run after the dog who turns and runs back to her, I watch her father walk with his head down, lost in his own thoughts.

Chapter Nine
Jensen

"Mila, be careful," I tell her as she runs down the beach. I know we are passing the white house, and I also know they finished everything last night. No one knows I went there last night after I knew everyone was gone. I went to take one last walk-through. I said goodbye to the memories, goodbye to the ghost. I also dropped off the papers to my grandmother, selling her the house for a penny. I don't want it. I don't want anything to do with it, so it's now hers.

I sat in that living room, looking into the fireplace as I burned all the pictures Julia and I had ever taken. Alone with a bottle of scotch.

Norma, Julia's mother, gets to spend one weekend a month with Mila. After Julia left me, her mother pleaded and begged for her to come back home, but Julia was not going to do that. Plus, Julia had just found out she was pregnant, and this time, it really couldn't have been mine. Besides, they were building their empire.

Scott was setting up his own construction company, and Julia took care of the paperwork.

Two months after Julia left, I received the divorce papers as well as the papers relinquishing her parental right to Mila. My attorney got her name taken off the birth certificate to make sure she could never come back for custody. I knew she wouldn't, but I covered my bases anyway. Norma begged me to let her be a part of Mila's life, and I agreed, with the condition that she is not to discuss Julia. There was no reason to talk to my girl about a mother who deserted us. Who deserted her own daughter. No daughter should grow up with the knowledge that not even her own mother wanted her. It was my one rule, and until she broke it, she could be in her life.

Now, I watch as my little girl smiles every single day; she is surrounded by so much love that she doesn't miss anything. I know she will have questions when she gets older, so I kept one picture of Julia. The one right after she gave birth with tears running down her face. I brought it home with me and slipped it in the bottom of my dresser drawer. One day, I'm going to have to answer where her mom is, and I hope this makes her feel loved even though she left her.

"Poppa, look, a bottle," she says as she points at an empty bottle of beer that has washed up on the shore. She picks up the branch lying next to it and throws it into the shallow water. Flounder jumps into the water and catches it, carrying it back out.

We walk a bit more until we circle around to head

home. I make Mila her Sunday night special of fish sticks and tater tots. I'm taking the pan out of the oven when my front door slams shut. "Uncle Gabe," Mila says from her spot on the couch as she watches *The Boss Baby*. Gabe is my cousin; our fathers are brothers. We grew up together, and he's like a brother to me, which is why Mila calls him Uncle. "Hi." He smiles at her and kisses her head.

I watch him walk into the kitchen from the huge family room. The open concept was the perfect decision. "What's got into you?" I ask him as I flip the fish sticks over and put them back in the oven. I watch Gabe go to the liquor cabinet and pour himself two fingers of scotch. Downing it, he then pours himself another two fingers. Once he finishes the second one, he stands there with his head hung. "So are we discussing this, or are you just going to sulk in the corner?" I ask him.

"I just met the woman replacing Laura," he says, and I stand there as I whisper, "Oh." Laura was Gabe's head nurse at the medical clinic; she was best friends with Bethany, their office manager. Bethany started off working together with Gabe, and it slowly progressed to them dating and getting engaged. I've never seen him happier. He had me build his dream house, but little did he know, she was going to be a runaway bride. He stood at the alter waiting for her to walk down as their families looked on, only to get the news she took off. She was offered a sales position in Chicago for a medical company. So just like that, Bethany was gone. It also didn't help that she got his best nurse Laura a job at the hospital. Not only was his fiancée gone, but she had also taken her best friend with her. Now, don't get me wrong, it's the biggest one for four towns over. We have people coming from all over just have Gabe treat them, but he refuses to move to the city and he refuses to give in to the hospitals. Instead, he does what he wants to for him.

"Yeah, that," he says as he sits on the stool at the island while I stand on the other side. "Plus, she lives in your old fucking house."

"Don't even fucking think about it." I point at him, and I'm not even sure I know what I'm threatening him about. "She doesn't need you sniffing around her just to add another name to that list of yours."

He looks at me like I have two heads. "What the fuck are you talking about? You know Crystal?"

"Oh, her." I cross my hands over my chest. "I thought you were talking about Hailey."

"And if I was?" he asks. His eyebrow goes up in challenge, so I change the subject.

"Why are you so pissed about it?"

"She wants to place her bed in the middle of the room. Diagonally," he says, gesturing with his hands. "Who does that?"

"So you fired her?" I ask, trying not to laugh at him.

"Yes, but then the little, the little," he says, trying to come up with a name, "the little woman called my father and quit."

Now I don't even try to hide the smile. Instead, I belly laugh out loud. "It's not fucking funny. I had to apologize to her."

I put my hand in front of my mouth and gasp. "You did?"

"Fuck you, Walker," he says. "I knew she was fucking trouble from the minute I got her application. She comes from one of the top hospitals in the US. She was even given a reference from the head of surgery, who called and begged me to turn her down." He gets up, getting more scotch. "I told my father to turn her down, told my father it wasn't a good idea, but then Grams came in, and it was a done deed."

"Why would she want to leave a big hospital for a small medical clinic?" I ask him. The oven beeps, and I turn to take the fish sticks out of the oven and place them on Mila's small plastic plate. I get the ketchup out and squeeze a bit on the plate. "Mila, come eat, honey."

"Okay, Poppa," she says, jumping off the couch and walking over to the island. She tries to climb up, but instead, Gabe picks her up and places her down. "I could've done it, Uncle Gabe."

"I know, but I didn't want you to fall down and do a big boo-boo," he says.

My little girl rolls her eyes at him. "I'm a big girl now."

"Yes, you are," I say to her. "Now, make sure you blow, okay, because they just came out of the oven." I push the plate in front of her as Gabe steals a tater tot.

"From what my father said, she came down with Hailey," Gabe says. Mila butts into our conversation.

"I like Hailey; she calls me Princess Mila," she says as she grabs a tater tot, dipping it in the ketchup, then she blows and bites a piece off. "She looks like a princess," Mila says as I just nod and try not to let my thoughts go back to the look sadness on her face the minute I opened my mouth and mentioned her husband.

"Eat because it's almost bath time," I tell her as she eats all her fish sticks. "You want to hang out while I put Mila to bed?" I ask Gabe. He nods his head and heads to the living room to sit on the couch, changing the TV to the sports channel while I take Mila back for a bath and story time.

Forty-five minutes later, I finally return to find Gabe sleeping on the couch. I turn off the television and make my way to my bedroom. I turn on the baby monitor, then peel off my shirt and finally get into the shower. I stand there in my big walk-in shower and let the hot water rain down on me. I close my eyes, thinking of the week ahead, but instead, I picture the beach, the waves, or better yet, the woman watching the waves.

My dreams play tricks on me that night as I toss and turn. I only wake when I get kneed in the balls by Mila, who climbed into my bed sometime during the night. I groan and look at the clock, 5:30 a.m. I roll off the bed and catch my breath as I hold my balls. Sliding my jogging pants on, I go to the kitchen to make a cup of coffee. Gabe's gone, so he must have taken off sometime in the middle of the night. I grab the coffee and sit at the island, looking outside. The whole back wall of my house has a panoramic view of the ocean. I'm about to take a sip of coffee when I see blond hair, and my head whips up. It's blowing as she walks down the beach wrapped in a blanket. When she gets to the steps that lead to my house, Flounder runs down and jumps on her. I rush outside and yell, "Flounder." I see that she is on her back now with the blanket off her and her cup of coffee tossed in the sand. Flounder sits on her and licks her face as if she is a treat.

"No." She tosses her head from right to left. "Stop, fuck." She tries to push him away, but he thinks it's a game and continues to lick her face while she squeezes her eyes shut. "Fuck off."

"Flounder." I issue the command, and he stops right away. She opens her eyes and rolls to her knees. I take in her cotton pjs as she picks up the blanket and shakes the sand off it. "What the fuck were you doing?" I ask her as she bends to grab her cup. She whips her head up to look at me.

"Me?" she says she dusts the sand from her back. "Your dog attacked me while I was walking on the beach."

"He doesn't like people on his property," I say as I pet his head, and he lies next to me.

"I'm sorry. Since when is a public beach your property?" she says and then puts up her hand. "You know what? Fuck that. Keep your dog leashed or I'm calling animal control next time." She turns to walk away.

"For what? Licking your face." I smirk at her and see her take in my shirtless chest.

"Licking my face?" she shrieks out, then lifts her shirt. I see that she is bleeding and her shirt is torn. "He bit me."

I want to see if she is okay, but I stop when she turns. "I'd better not need a tetanus shot." She opens the blanket again and drapes it over her shoulders, then she walks away.

"Flounder, that wasn't nice," I tell him as he tilts his head to the side and looks at me. "Not nice." When I look up, she's already gone. I go inside just in time for Mila to come into the kitchen. "Poppa, can I have Lucky Charms?" I nod, picking her up and kissing her sleepy face. She wraps her arms around my neck and lays her head on my shoulder, and we sit on the couch lost in our own thoughts.

Chapter Ten
Hailey

I storm up the steps and walk straight into my bedroom, scratching my head because it was itchy from all the sand in my hair. After deciding to take an early morning walk, I was enjoying the sound of the crashing waves and emptying my mind. It was the first time in a long time that I just had a blank thought until I looked up and saw that fucking dog launching himself at me. My first instinct was to cover my face, which is when he snipped at my shirt, tearing it, and I felt the burning right away. I tried to push him away, but he thought it was a fucking game. I toss the blanket in the wash along with my pjs, making my way to the bathroom and the hot shower. When I finally feel like I have no more sand in hair, I put on a pair of leggings and a loose shirt and make my way to the kitchen. This time, Crystal is up and dressed in her scrubs. She looks up from her toast as she takes me in. "What the heck happened to you?" she asks as I shake my head, pouring a cup of coffee.

"Fucking dog attacked me this morning when I was taking a walk." I raise my hand for her to see my battle wound. She comes closer and takes my wrist to examine the wound.

"He tore the skin. You'd better hope he's had all his shots," she says as she walks back to her toast and bites off another piece.

"I don't think he would put his daughter in danger like that," I say, not mentioning his name. "Asshole. Blamed me." I sit down with my cup of coffee and open my laptop. "As if he owns the fucking beach."

"What time did you go for a walk?" she asks as she looks at the clock. "It's only seven?"

"I couldn't sleep," I tell her as I click open my email. "It's getting better but …" I shrug as I try to forget what I want to say.

"Okay, I have to go," she says, picking up her bag. "You have bail money saved up in case, right?" she asks as she takes the keys to my car.

"I have you covered. Now, can you try not to kill him?" I smile at her as my email finally stops pinging. Pick up my laptop, I make my way to my bedroom and outside where I sit in the swing. By the time I look up, it's three p.m. and my stomach is growling. Time for a break.

I grab an apple and make my way to the beach to sit down and watch the water. The water is calmer today, the wind almost nonexistent. I gaze into the distance at the water that seemingly never ends. I look down the beach and see Mila running with the dog. But her father isn't trailing her this time. Instead, a woman I've never seen watches as Mila runs and the dog knocks into her as she tries to steady herself. She doesn't get a chance before the dog comes running back and knocks her off her feet. She flies through the air, landing on her side, and her cries echo off the empty beach. I'm sprinting down the beach and make it to her before the woman does, falling to my knees beside her. "Mila, honey, are you okay?" I ask her as I pick her up and place her on my lap, where she's holding her wrist.

The woman finally makes it to us. "Mila, honey, are you okay?" I look up at this woman and glare at her while Flounder comes over and lies down near her feet, putting his paw on her as she cries. The woman tries to take Mila from my arms, and she wails even louder, so I turn my body as I get to my feet.

"Where is Jensen?" I ask the woman who stands with her hands on her mouth. I carry Mila to Jensen's house, and as we are walking up the steps, Mila starts sobbing again, holding her wrist. "We need to get her to the doctor," I say as I walk in the open door. Another woman in the kitchen throws the towel that she is folding down and races over. "We need to get her to the doctor. The dog knocked her off her feet, and she landed on her arm," I tell the woman who just nods as she walks to the counter to grab her purse and keys. She also tries to take Mila, who shakes her head and burrows herself deeper against my chest.

"Norma." The lady talks to the one who was on the

beach. "You need to move your car, so I can get out."

The woman looks at me now, up and down. "I think I can handle this without a stranger holding my grand-daughter," she says to me with a snide leer.

"Listen, lady, I don't know who you are, or what is going on right now, but if you don't move your car, I'm going to ram it out of my way," I say. The lady next to me stands straight, looking at Norma, who just walks outside, gets in her car, and takes off.

"What the hell is her problem?" I look down and find Mila looking at me. "Are you okay, Princess Mila?"

She shakes her head as we walk outside and get into the car. "I'm going to have to tie you in your seat so you're safe, okay?" I tell her as I place her in her chair, and she wails out the minute her arm is moved, and it just plops down. "Okay, okay," I say as I pick her back up. "New plan," I say as I get inside with her on my lap. Wrapping one arm around her, I manage to buckle myself in. "Sorry but you need to hurry up please," I tell the lady driving as I look down at Mila. My heart breaks for the pain in her eyes, so I lean down and kiss her head. "You are so brave, Mila. So, so brave."

She closes her eyes and dozes off, and the lady drives us to the clinic right next door to Jensen's office. "I'm going to take her in," I tell the lady. "You need to run over and get her father." I walk into the clinic while she runs to Jensen's office. I get to the counter, and I'm about to talk to the lady behind the desk when I see Crystal and tears run down my face. "She got hurt," I say. I try not to move her, but she whimpers out in pain while she sleeps.

Opening the door, Crystal waits for me to walk in, then starts issuing orders to the other nurses. "Someone get Gabe." I follow her to a room, and she asks me, "What happened?"

"I was sitting outside eating an apple because my eyes were hurting from the computer, and I saw her and that fucking dog playing." I look down as Mila opens her eyes, and I smile at her. "She got hurt, but she was so brave," I say as I try not to lose my shit.

"I think it's her shoulder or her wrist." I look at Crystal who comes over and looks at Mila.

"Hey, Princess Mila, you think I could see what is wrong with you?" she asks Mila as she looks at me with fear in her eyes.

"I'm not going anywhere. I promise I'll be right here, but Crystal needs to check and see what's wrong, okay?" I say. Once she nods, I walk to the examination table and place her on it. Her arm just flops down, and the bone in her wrist is crooked. When Crystal grasps her wrist lightly, she cries out, and I sit next to her head.

"Look at me, Princess, just … I know it hurts, but I promise you she will make it okay."

"Don't cry, Hailey," Mila says. "I won't cry if you don't cry." I nod my head just as Gabe walks into the room.

"What the fuck is going on?" he says as he takes in Mila on the table. "Where did all this blood come from?" he asks. I look at him in confusion and then look at the floor and see that the blood is from my feet.

NATASHA MADISON

"It's from Hailey," Crystal tells him as she looks at me. "She probably cut her feet, and with the adrenaline, she didn't notice."

I look at my feet, and the burning suddenly breaks through, but I don't notice it till Gabe talks. "Her shoulder is dislocated," he says just as Jensen runs into the room, his face white as a ghost.

"Mila," he whispers as he takes in the scene. "Mila, honey. Poppa is here." He comes to my side as he gets down and kisses her nose. "What happened?"

Gabe talks because my tongue has suddenly swelled in my mouth and doesn't move. "Flounder crashed into Mila, and Hailey is bleeding all over my floor." Jensen looks down at my bloody feet.

"I was sitting on the beach, and then she was there with …" I shake my head, not even remembering the name of the woman.

"I was with Grammy Norma," Mila says. "It hurts, Poppa."

"Okay, folks, I have to put her shoulder back in place." He looks at Jensen. "It's going to hurt, and she will cry, but there is nothing we can do about it."

"Okay," Jensen says and looks down at Mila. I get up and start to walk away to give them their own time, but Mila shouts out for me.

"You stay with me, Hailey," she says as she looks at me with big tears in her eyes, and I nod my head as tears escape the side of my eye. "You promised."

"I'm not going anywhere," I tell her as I stand next to the table. "It's going to hurt," I tell her, "but how

102

about we get some ice cream after?" I talk to her while Gabe and Crystal set everything out. Gabe nods for me to keep talking to her as he goes on the other side and takes her arm in his hand. "What is your favorite flavor?" I ask her, trying not to look at what Gabe is doing, but she doesn't answer because he snaps it back in place. She yells out in pain, and I sob, putting my hand to my mouth to stop it.

"All done," Gabe says, then looks at Jensen and me. "She is going to need X-rays for the wrist, but by looking at it, I can say it's broken, so she is going to need a cast." Her sobs slowly start to stop.

"You were so brave, Princess," I tell her as I squat down eye to eye with her.

"It hurt just a little bit." Mila picks up her good hand as she pinches her finger and thumb together.

"You can go now. She just needs her family, not a stranger." I hear from beside me. I look over, not meeting his eyes, since all he does is look at his daughter.

"Mila, I need to go and have Crystal look at my feet now, okay? I'll come back and see you later."

"Okay," Mila says as she looks at me and then her father. I lean down and kiss her head before turning and walking out of the room.

Chapter Eleven
Jensen

Every Monday, I usually do my turn of visiting the job sites to make sure we're on time and especially on budget. I only just got back to the office after lunch and was sitting at my desk when Jessica, the nanny/cleaning lady/cook who comes in every Monday, Tuesday, and Thursday, called and told me Norma was there to visit and they were going to go for a walk on the beach. I didn't think anything of it till about thirty minutes later when I heard Jessica running in yelling for me.

"Walker," she yelled out hysterically. I flew out of my chair and ran to the front where she was standing with tears pouring down her face. "Mila."

I stood there in place, my heart sinking to my stomach as fear seeped into my bones. "She's next door." Not even listening to anything else she was saying, I ran past her, my lungs burning as I prayed to every single god that I thought would listen to keep my baby safe. I was beside myself with worry, I had just walked in and saw my baby crying on an exam table, with her arm hanging lip. I didn't know what else to do so I blamed the one person who was in front of me, Hailey. I was mean and rude, dismissing her like she didn't just put my daughter before herself.

"I guess your daughter gets her all her manners from her mother," Crystal hisses right before she walks out the room, and Gabe whistles.

"I would think that is a direct hit," he says and shakes his head. "You do realize that Hailey carried your daughter in here while she bled, right? She didn't even know she was bleeding. The only thing she cared about was Mila."

"Is that all?" I tell him, my eyes never leaving my daughter who sleeps on the examining table. Gabe turns and walks out, and I think of how this day went from okay to more fucked than I can explain.

I watch Mila as she whimpers in her sleep. As I lean my hip on the table, one of the nurses comes in with a mop and cleans up Hailey's blood from the floor. "Oh, my gosh," my mother says from the doorway. "Whose blood is that?" she asks. She looks like she is going to faint.

"It's not Mila's," I tell her as she enters the room and comes to the table. Looking down at Mila, she wipes away tears too. "My poor baby, what happened?" she asks, looking at me.

"From what I understand, they were walking on the beach and Flounder knocked her over by accident." At least, that is what I got from the bits and pieces everyone's told me.

"Okay," Crystal says as she walks back in the room, her shoes squeaking on the wet floor. "We need to take her for an X-ray." She doesn't look at me but smiles at my mother. "Glad we got Hailey's blood cleaned up," she says. My mother looks at me with her eyes going into slits as she folds her hands over her chest. "You can pick her up and carry her," Crystal says, so I lean down and pick her up, cradling her in my arms, and follow her down the hall.

"I'll wait here," my mother says to us, turning to go back to the front of the office. Crystal opens the door to the X-ray room as I place Mila on the table, and her eyes flicker open.

"Poppa," she whispers as she looks around. "Where is Hailey?"

"Hailey," Crystal says as she brings over a blue heavy vest, "is getting stitches." She places the vest on top of Mila. "This is heavy," she says as she lifts her arm and sets her broken wrist on the side of her. "But it's to make sure we only take pictures of your arm." She smiles at her.

"Why does Hailey need stitches?" Mila asks first thing.

"Well," Crystal says as she places a gray square under her arm, bringing the X-ray machine down over her wrist, "she cut her feet on a bottle, and it was very deep. But don't worry, she is all better. Now see that glass over there." She points at the plexiglass in the corner of the room. "I'm going to go in there with your dad while we take pictures." She brushes Mila's hair away from her face. "You are very, very brave." She smiles at Mila then glares at me. "Go stand over there." Her bedside manner vanishes.

I go to the corner and stand there while Crystal comes and presses a couple of buttons, then goes back and moves the machine to a different position. After taking about five different shots, she looks at them and walks back to Mila, taking the blue cover off her. "All done, Princess Mila." I walk out and go over to her. I pick her up and carry her back to the room, where my mother sits with her legs crossed as she rocks her foot.

"Oh, there is my girl," she says as she gets up, rushing to us and kissing Mila's forehead.

"I fell, and Hailey got stiches on her feet," she informs my mother, who just nods. I place Mila down on the table as my mother grabs her phone and puts on YouTube for her.

"I sent Jessica home. She drove Hailey home as well."

"Not now, Mom, please. Just." I beg her to drop it, so she nods. "Let's talk later."

"Okay, folks," Gabe says as he walks into the room. "Hey, Auntie." He goes to the computer, opening it and typing something as the X-rays come on the screen. "Clean break. Good news is it isn't her growth plate, and it should heal in no time." He turns to look at Mila. "Now, what color cast do you want? We have blue, yellow, green, pink, or camo."

"Pink," Mila yells. "Uncle Gabe, I'm getting ice

cream with Hailey," she says. Gabe just nods his head.

"Aren't you the lucky one, but I think Hailey left so she could go home and rest. She got ten stiches on her foot, so I sent her home to sleep."

Mila looks from Gabe to me. "We need to bring Hailey ice cream."

"We'll see, baby girl. How about we just get you fixed first?"

"Okay," she says, happy with that while Gabe laughs and prepares to start wrapping her cast.

"It's a waterproof cast, but try to keep it as dry as possible, and I will see her in four weeks," Gabe says as he kisses Mila and walks out of the room.

"I don't know about you, Mila, but I'm ready to go home and watch *The Boss Baby*," my mother says, and Mila nods her head. I pick her up and carry her outside as she shows everyone her pink cast.

We make it home, and we camp out on the couch while my mother fixes everything else. Mila finally falls asleep in my arms as I'm watching *The Secret Life of Pets* for the second time, so I lay her down in bed. "Did you give her some Tylenol for the pain?" my mother asks me as soon as I come out of Mila's room.

"I did," I tell her as I sit on the couch and rub my neck. "Let's hear it." I look over at her as she turns off the television and turns to me.

"Jessica called me the minute she walked Mila into the room to tell me the whole story. Do you know that she ran down the beach, no shoes, over shards of glass?" She puts her hands up. "Obviously, she didn't see the smashed bottles, but nothing would have stopped her from getting to Mila."

I look at her, the shock seeping in. "I didn't know all that."

"Well, now you do. But even if you hadn't, how dare you treat someone like that? Especially after she put your daughter's needs in front of hers."

"I didn't ask her to do that," I say, now getting up to start pacing.

"You didn't have to. She would have done it for anyone else."

"I don't know what she told you, but I didn't ask her for anything."

"She isn't the enemy here," she says softly.

"What, and I am?" I place my hands on my hips. "Mila had Jessica and Norma by her; she didn't need Hailey."

My mother shakes her head, getting up. "Yes, and where is Norma?" she asks looking around. "Because it appears she hightailed it pretty fast."

"Look, I don't want to argue with you."

"I'm not arguing with you, Jensen. I'm telling you what you did to that girl was unacceptable, and if it was my daughter, well, you can bet your ass I'd be breaking down your door." She comes up to me, and she puts her hand on my cheek. "Stop punishing her for what Julia did."

I roll my eyes at her. "I'm not punishing her for any-thing. Why do I have to like her?"

"You don't have to do anything, but you need to

let go of that chip you have on your shoulder when it comes to her."

"Fine. I'll be more civil," I tell her, and she nods her head at me.

"Good. I'll see myself out," she says. She turns to grab her things and waves as I walk her out the door. I turn off the lights before going to Mila's room and checking on her. Her cover already kicked off her, she's also tossed the pillow I'd propped under her arm to the floor. My dreams are foggy all night long, the only thing staying the same is the storm brewing in the back.

Chapter Twelve
Hailey

"It's so itchy," I whine to Crystal two days after the whole ordeal.

I had no idea I was even bleeding when I walked into the clinic. The only thing on my mind was getting Mila help and having her stop crying.

When I finally left her, I went into another room. Sitting down, I look down at my now dirty black feet, the blood dripping from my left foot. "Idiot," Crystal says as she walks in. "Put your feet up." I did as she told me, and I hiss from the burning as she cleans them. "You're going to need a shot and stitches for sure," she says as she assesses the bottom of my foot. Gabe walks in.

"There she is, wonder woman." He smiles as Crystal glares at him. "Hey." He raises his arms in surrender. "I'm not the bad guy."

"Whatever," she says as she gathers the supplies to

start the stitches.

"How is Mila?" I ask him as Crystal prepares to give me a shot to numb it. "Motherfucker, that hurts."

"She's fine. Listen, about my cousin," he starts to say, but I raise my hand to stop him.

"Don't even bother." That's all I say because then I start to hiss under my breath as Crystal works on my foot. Gabe walks back out of the room.

She bandages me up and says, "I'm going to get you some crutches for home because you shouldn't put any pressure on it. Emma, the other nurse, will come in. I have to get Mila in for her X-rays," she says as she walks out.

"Great," I say as the throbbing in my foot starts. Emma comes in with the crutches, and as I grab them from her, I ask, "Will you be able to call me a taxi?"

"Jessica will drive you." I hear from the side of the room and look to find Heidi. "Are you okay?" she asks as she blinks away tears.

"I'm fine. It was just a little cut." I try not to make it bigger than it was.

"A cut that needed ten stitches," Emma added. "But who's counting? Excuse me." She walks out.

"Is Mila okay?" I ask her and then look down. "I know it's not my place but ..."

"It is your place. You put that little girl before your own safety. Thank you."

"It was nothing, but I did promise her ice cream, so if you could get her some, that would be great," I say as I walk past her on my crutches. "Good thing I work

from home, right?" I smile and walk into the waiting room where the woman Jessica is waiting for me.

"Jessica, I'm assuming?" I take in her disheveled hair, her eyes still wet with tears as she wrings a tissue in her hand. She walks up to me and grabs me in a hug so forcefully, I almost fall back. "Thank you," she whispers. I just smile at her. "Let's get you home."

She drops me off at home where I plop down on the couch and don't move.

Now, two days later, I'm ready to rip the bandage off. "I think I'm suffering from cabin fever," I tell Crystal as she walks around the kitchen, packing her lunch and grabbing her things for work.

"Just eight more days," Crystal sings as she kisses my head and walks out. I flip her the bird as I get up and make my way to the back. I sit in the swing as I watch the ocean and do my work. I'm about to make myself something to eat when I hear a knock on the door.

I get up, grabbing my crutches, and walk to my front door as the knocking continues. "Coming," I shout. When I get to the door and open it, I see Heidi, Delores, and Mila.

"Hailey," Mila yells happily as she bounces in. "We brought you presents," she says happily.

"You did?" I drop the crutches as I get on my knee to give her a hug. "How is my Princess Mila?" I say as I take in her pink cast. "Does it hurt?" She shakes her head while I try to get up and hop on one foot to the table. "Sorry, guys, I'm a klutz with those two metal sticks."

Delores walks in with her arms filled with bags while Heidi picks up the crutches and carries in a vase filled with tulips.

Mila waits by my side. Grabbing my hand, she looks up at me and smiles. And at that moment, I know I would do anything for this little girl. Her heart is pure even though her father is an asshole. "Let's go see what all the fuss is about." I smile at her. She nods and patiently holds my hand while I hop to the kitchen. She hops with me, thinking it's a fun joke. Her giggles fill the house, making my heart happy. I pull out a chair and plop down in it. Closing my laptop, I put it aside while Mila pulls out the chair next to me.

Delores comes over with a bag. "We thought this might help the recovery time." She hands me the bag. Mila gets on her knees on her chair and claps her hands together in excitement.

I look over at her. "Do you want to help me open this?" Her face lights up even more as she nods her head, so I push away from the table to give her space to climb into my lap. She grabs the bag and pulls out a box. "What do we have here?" I ask her as she takes in the box in her hand.

"It's chocolate," she says as I look down. "We can share it." She tilts her head and smiles up at me.

I tap her nose with my finger. "You would share my chocolate with me?" I ask, and she nods her head. "You are a great helper. What else is in there?"

She takes out what looks like a spa basket. "Soap." She just shrugs while I inspected the loofah, bubble bath, bath salts, and a couple of bath bombs.

"That is for after the stitches come out for you to sit and enjoy," Delores says when I finally look up and see Heidi in the kitchen making coffee for us.

"I will use this as soon as I can," I tell them while Mila pulls out magazines from the bag. "Oh, my favorite." I grab the *Cosmopolitan* and flip through it.

"That's all; all gone," Mila says as she pushes the bag to the side. "Now my turn." She claps her hand as Heidi brings over the small bag. "I buy all this for you," Mila says as she hands me the bag, and my hand goes to my chest.

"All for me?" I ask her as I open it and take out her gifts to me one at a time. "Crayons, coloring books, a puzzle, oh, and what is this?" I ask as I admire a picture that looks like she drew.

"It's me and you on the beach." She points out her and me—my body bigger than anything else with two stick legs. "When you are all better, we can go look for seashells."

With the picture in my hand, I focus on the two of us, and the dreaded feeling I've lived with for so long is now dull. I don't know when it happened, but at that moment, my heart doesn't hurt. Not even when I think about when Eric and I walked down the beach, picking up our own seashells. "Do you want to?" she asks. I look up at Delores and Heidi, who have both stopped and are staring at me.

"Whenever you want to go, you tell me, and I'll bring a bucket where we can put them all inside." I smile through the tears that threaten to fall. "Thank you so much, guys, for all the presents, but you didn't have to."

Delores pats my hand as she shakes her head. "There isn't anything in the world that could thank you for what you did." I nod, unable to say anything over big lump in my throat, so I listen to Mila tell us a story about how she wants to be a mermaid.

They spend the rest of the hour with me. Heidi makes coffee, and I try to get up and serve them but am told to sit. So I take out the coloring book and color with Mila and discuss how the weather is changing and my plans for the weekend, which consists of ordering stuff for my office. They both ask if they can come with me, and even Mila says she wants to come, so we plan the shopping trip for Saturday. I hobble to the door to say goodbye to them and watch them drive off. Going back inside, I take my computer out back, where I sit on the swing and continue to work. But my mind is all over the place. The calmness of this place makes me think back to all my memories of Eric.

How come I didn't see all the signs he had another life? I close the laptop, knowing I'm not going to get anymore work done today. I sit there with my leg propped up on the swing as the past year of my life replays in my mind.

"I just got a call," he would say as he came downstairs with his bag already packed, "but I should be

back in a couple of days."

I never questioned anything. The calls he would make would never be at night, only during the day.

"I'm going to call you tomorrow. I will probably work through the night to make sure I finish earlier." I shake my head, thinking I was such an idiot

He only FaceTimed from his rental car, but was it even a rental? I try to think back to remember if the seats were the same color. *"The hotels have the worse Wi-Fi connections."*

How did I never suspect anything? How he couldn't keep his hands off me, attacking me the minute he came into the house. *"I can't get enough of you."*

The times we lay in bed late at night, both of us on our stomachs as we discussed our dreams. His dream to finally have a job where he didn't have to travel and to see me pregnant. My dream to finally be a mother to however many babies God wanted to give us.

"A penny for your thoughts." I hear from behind me. I turn around and see Crystal looking at me. "You look a million miles away."

I shake my head as I rub away a tear I didn't know was running down my cheek. "Just thinking," I tell her. She comes over to the swing, picks up my feet, and then sets them on her lap when she sits down. We swing and watch the waves crash into the sand. "You know if you think about it," I start, my eyes never leaving the water, "the signs were all there that something was going on." I laugh. "All there … I was just too blind to see."

"If you were blind, then I guess we all were. None of us suspected anything."

"But you guys didn't live with him." I inhale. "I was such a fool."

"No, you weren't." She tries to convince me I wasn't, but anger now replaces the pain I've felt for the past month.

"I hate him," I say, my eyes watching the buoy in the distance as it sways from side to side. "Like with my whole heart. For as much love as I had for him, I have just as much hatred." A tear slips down my face as I finally realize I will never have the answers I seek because I will never get a chance to confront him. I will never get that closure, and I will have to find that within myself. He may have left me with questions I have to look for in myself. Answers I have to come up with on my own.

"Hailey, you trusted him. You did what anyone else would have done." She rubs my legs as I stretch my arm out and lay my head down on it. "I went to see her," she whispers out as I look at her. "I didn't want to tell you ... I just." She takes a deep breath and looks over. "We went down and saw her."

"We?" I ask her, confused.

"Well, Blake wasn't going to let me go by myself, just in case I did something harsh." She shrugs, and I know exactly why Blake would go with her. "I just wanted to know, in case you had questions later. She ..." I sit looking at her and taking her in, my protector. Tears run down Crystal's face now. "She is so different from you. She isn't strong like you are. He's all she has ever known, and she had no idea. She didn't suspect for one minute he would do that to her, to his family. He always traveled for work, so it wasn't like a red flag or anything. The only thing that changed is that the FaceTimes got less and less at the end."

"They have kids," I say, and she nods her head.

"Yes, and every single day, she has to look into the eyes of her children and see the good in them or else she is going to go insane." She wipes tears from her own cheeks now. "That is what she has to live with. I wanted to hate her, to blame her for what he did to you, to us, but she had fewer answers than you did."

"I can't even imagine. I hated her," I start to say. "I hated that she had that with him. That she had him forever. That their love would go on forever in their children."

Crystal laughs sarcastically. "It was a lie. As much as you think your life was a lie, so was hers." I nod, and neither of us say anything as we watch the water go from dark blue to black as the sun sets and nighttime blankets the sky.

Chapter Thirteen
Jensen

Every day for the past two weeks, we've taken a walk on the beach. For the past fourteen days, I have walked past the house, forcing myself never to look up but failing each time. Hailey is never outside, and I don't even see movement in the house. Trust me, even Mila looks over to see if Hailey is there, and each day, she just says, "She can't come out with her boo-boo." She skips ahead, and I watch her as Flounder follows closely by her. He knows she's hurt, so he doesn't try to play with her.

"Poppa, can we go eat pizza?" Mila asks as she bends to pick up a seashell.

"Sure thing," I say. It's Friday, so why not? Plus, she's spending this weekend with Norma. After the whole beach thing, I wanted to say no, but I know it was an accident, and it could have happened to any one of us.

Walking into the office later that day, I make plans

to do stuff around the house to get it ready for summer. A knock on the door makes me look up. "Hey," I say as Kimberley saunters into the room.

"I'm about to head out," she says. I glance at the clock on the wall and see it's five o'clock. "Did you need me for anything?"

"No," I say, putting my papers away. "I think I'm going to call it a day too." I get up, and we walk out together. I look into Brody's office and see he is already gone. "Did everyone else leave?" I ask her as we walk to the front office.

"Yes," she says, looking down. "It's just the two of us." She smiles and tucks her hair behind her ear, giving my stomach an uneasy feeling. "Did you maybe want to get something to eat?"

"Umm." I back away just a bit. "Kimberley."

"I know you aren't big on dating," she starts, and I put up my hand to stop her.

"Kimberley, if I somehow gave you the wrong idea or impression, I'm sorry. But it …" She nods her head, grabs her bag, and walks out, only looking behind her before closing the door.

"What the fuck?" I say to myself as I look around, closing everything and locking up. I get home four minutes later, and Mila runs to jump into my arms, her cast hitting me in the head.

"Hey, baby girl." I kiss her neck. "Did you have fun with Grandma?" I ask. She nods, and my mother comes into the room.

"Oh good, you're home. I promised your grandmother I would come over and help her set up for the tea gathering she is having on Sunday." She grabs her purse, kisses Mila and then me, and then lets herself out.

"You ready to go get our pizza on, and then I was thinking we could go for a walk," I tell her, thinking of maybe taking a walk down Main Street.

"Let's go, Freddy," she says, wiggling herself out of my arms. I walk out the door with her and buckle her into her booster seat, kissing her nose. Getting behind the wheel of the truck, I start the car and "Despacito" comes on. I groan as Mila starts singing in the background. I pull out of my driveway and drive down the street, coming to a stop at the corner where I see blond hair right in front of me.

She walks with a little bit of a limp, but I know right away it's Hailey. I'm about to drive by, but Mila shrieks as she rolls down her window. "Hailey-bailey." My eyebrows pinch together as Hailey turns her head, and I take in her face. The darkness around her eyes is gone. Her face is a little bit fuller as is her body. Fuck, am I checking her out? I'm about to drive right past her, but she waves at Mila in the back, and I stay there stopped wondering what to do. "Hey there, Mila-fila," she jokes as she walks across the street, and I take her in a bit more. Her black tights mold to her lean legs with a simple V-neck t-shirt and a plaid sweater tied around her waist. Her black sneakers make the whole outfit. "What's up, Princess?" She continues to talk to Mila as I continue to watch her.

"Are you going for a walk?" she asks as I see Hailey switch from foot to foot.

"I am. I'm going down to get some pizza."

"We are going to eat pizza," Mila informs her. "You want to come with us?" I groan inwardly. Hailey looks at me, her smile falling, and then back at Mila.

"Um," she says, and I see her trying to come up with an excuse, but Mila doesn't give her a chance and neither does the car in back of me who honks.

"Get in," I say harsher than I want to, and Hailey just looks at me. If Mila wasn't there, I'm sure she would turn away and tell me to fuck off. "Please." But the horn honking again has her walking around the truck. She opens the back door and gets in on the passenger side next to Mila. I put the car in drive as we make our way to D'Amore; the girls chattering in the back make me grip the steering wheel tighter. I park the truck and get out, opening Mila's door to find her already unbuckled and climbing out on Hailey's side. They walk around the truck hand in hand while Mila tells her about the afternoon she had with my mother.

We walk in, and the hostess asks me how many. I say three, but Hailey tells her that she is going to order for takeout. "You aren't going to eat with us?" Mila asks as Hailey looks from the hostess and then back at Mila.

"Okay fine, three," she says as the hostess brings us to the only available table with three seats. It's at the end of the table with one seat on one side and then two on the other side. Mila walks to the single seat while

Hailey walks around the table and sits down, waiting for me to sit down also.

The chairs are so close together that our legs are touching, and the heat from her leg seeps into me. "What can I get for you guys?" the waitress asks. Mila says, "Apple juice. Hailey, you want one too?"

"Sure, I'll have an apple juice. You want pepperoni, Mila, or did you want to have the cheese like we had yesterday?" I look at Hailey.

"When?" I ask her, and she looks at me. Finally, for the first time, our eyes meet. The look in them cloudy, stormy, like she is fighting something again.

"We had lunch yesterday at my house," she informs me quietly as the waitress waits for the rest of the order.

"We will have cheese with three apple juices," I tell her, then she grabs the menus from us. "So when did this lunch happen?"

"I have to go potty," Mila says. I start to get up, but Hailey is already on her feet, looking at me.

"I can take her to the women's one. If it's okay." Mila holds her hand while Hailey looks at me, and I just nod. After they turn around and walk to the back, the waitress appears with the apple juices. Fuck, what I would give for a beer. They come back laughing a couple of minutes later. Hailey picks up Mila and places her on her chair.

"So you guys had lunch?" I don't let her change the subject as Hailey nods.

"We had pizza, and then we went on a mission,"

Mila tells me. "We found fifty-eight seashells."

Hailey crosses her legs, the coldness from her separation now getting to my leg. "Sixty-two." She grabs her juice and takes a sip. The waitress brings some crayons for Mila. She says thank you and turns over her placemat to color.

"Your mother comes over sometimes with Hailey during the week for lunch," she says softly from beside me, her thumbs hitting the table nervously. "I finally got my stitches out and could walk or at least limp. It's still tender when I put too much pressure on it."

"Then why the fuck were you walking here?" I ask her, angry that she is not listening to orders.

"Um …" she says, taken aback by my harsh tone. "Crystal left this morning for her weekend retreat, and she took my car," she says, looking down, then up again. "Besides, I wanted to get some fresh air."

"You shouldn't put that much pressure on it if it hurts. It will most likely take longer to heal," I tell her as I hear a voice being cleared beside me. Turning, I come face to face with Norma.

"Grandma Norma," Mila says as she waves. "We are having pizza," she informs her.

"I see that," she says as she looks over at Hailey. "Who is your friend?" Her voice drips with accusations, and my spine goes straight.

"This is Hailey," I tell her. "The one who carried Mila down the beach the day of the accident."

Norma looks over at her and just smirks. "I didn't realize you two knew each other personally." That pisses me off, but it makes Hailey start to get up.

"I should go," she starts, and I see that her chest is moving fast now. "I'm not feeling well." But I grab her hand before she stands all the way up.

"No." I raise my voice a touch and look over at her. "We are going to eat pizza." I look back at Norma, asking her, "Is that all?"

She nods at me and then leans down to kiss Mila. "I will see you tomorrow. I have everything ready for our mani-pedi party." This makes Mila squeal and clap her hands. She walks away from us, not stopping, and heads straight out the front door. The waitress arrives and places the pizza in front of us. I grab a slice to cut up for Mila. Looking over at Hailey, I see her just sitting there, blinking at her empty plate.

"Eat." I place a slice of pizza on her plate, prompting her to look up at me.

"I'm not hungry," she says quietly. "I really don't feel well." Her face has gone from happy two seconds ago to ash white. Her eyes blink furiously, and I know Mila does the same thing when she tries to be brave and not cry. I place the plate in front of Mila, and she grabs her fork and starts eating.

"I'm sorry about Norma," I tell her quietly. "That was uncalled for." I look at Mila to make sure she isn't listening to us. "Please eat." The plea leaves my mouth before I can snatch it back.

She shakes her head. "I …" She looks over and is about to tell me something when Luigi comes over.

"Hey, if it isn't my two favorite girls," he says as he

winks at Mila and then smiles at Hailey. "I didn't see you guys come in."

"You must have been busy, but I was just going to head out," Hailey says as she stands, and I see her wince. "I think I overdid it with the walking today." She smiles at Luigi and then hobbles to Mila's side. "I'm going to go home now. My foot hurts a little." Mila nods at her as she leans in to kiss Hailey's cheek. "I'll see you next week for another treasure hunt." She smiles at us as she says bye, and I watch as she limps out the door.

"She's a beauty, that one," Luigi says. I just glare at him.

"Don't even think about it," I tell him. I'm not sure why since it's not my business. I get up and say, "Mila, wait here with Luigi. I'm going to tell Hailey we will bring the pizza to her house." I run out and look down the street to see her limping her way down Main Street, her head down, shoulders slumped. I jog up to her, startling her. "Hailey."

Her hand flies to her chest. "Jesus fuck, you scared me," she says as I look at her and see the tears that have been washed away.

"Are you hurt?" I ask her, looking at her foot. "Sit down," I tell her as I direct her to the chair right in front of the hairdresser's. I don't wait for her to answer. "I'm going to go get Mila, and we can eat at my house," I tell her as she shakes her head.

"I just want to go home," she says as she looks down at her foot.

"Okay, fine," I say, combing my hands through my hair. "Let me go get Mila, and I'll take you home."

"You don't have to do that," she says, but I just walk away from her. The pain in her eyes is too much to bear right now as my thoughts start their own war. Part of me just says fuck it let her go, but the bigger part tells me to help her. I walk back in and find Luigi with Mila and the pizza already boxed.

"I boxed it up for you and explained to Mila that Hailey would need a lift home." I grab the box from him and pick up Mila.

"Where is Hailey, Poppa?" she asks me as she wraps an arm around my neck, and I carry her out to my truck.

"She is waiting in front of Auntie Darla's shop," I tell her as I buckle her in and get in, hoping she waited for me. When I pull up, Hailey looks up, and I can see the tears are gone. She gets up and walks to the truck, smiling at Mila, but the smile is fake and forced.

"You don't feel good?" Mila asks Hailey as she gets in the back seat, avoiding me.

"No, Princess." As soon as she buckles her seat belt, I drive off and head toward the white house. I pull up and see that the lights outside are on. A soft light from inside shines through the front windows. She unbuckles the seat belt as soon as I put the car in park, and Mila unbuckles her own. "What are you going?" she asks Mila.

"We have to take care of Hailey. She's sick," Mila says.

"Oh no, honey. I'm going to be okay." She tucks Mila's hair behind her ears. "I just need to rest."

"That's okay. We can watch a movie. It's movie night." Mila says as she looks at me over the seat. "Right, Poppa?"

I look back at her and then at Hailey. This girl with a heart of gold looks at me, waiting for me to do the right thing. I almost tell her no—it almost comes out of my mouth—but I can't let her down. "Sure thing, angel," I say as I get out. I open the door to take Mila out, but once again, Hailey already has her in her arms. I walk over as Hailey carries Mila up the steps and walks into her house.

"Do you have Netflix?" Mila asks Hailey as she smiles at her. "It's Netflix and chill."

"Um." Hailey laughs and then looks at me. "If only she knew what that really meant." I put my hand in front of my mouth to hide my smile as she walks to the couch.

"I'm going to potty," Mila says as she walks into the hallway; the fact she is so familiar with this house has me asking myself all types of questions.

"You really don't have to stay," she says as she looks down at her hands and then up again. "I know you don't like being here," she says and then whispers, "or me," then speaks louder, "so I can just tell her that I'm going to bed."

"I don't know you, so I can't even say if I like you or not," I tell her to clarify that I don't not like her. "And this house is a sore spot for me," I tell her as I put my hands on my hips and finally take a minute to look around and see the furniture she picked out. It feels so much like a home. Even when we lived here, it was still missing that home feeling. I don't have time to think because Mila comes skipping back in.

"Did you wash your hands?" Hailey asks. Mila smirks and then turns back to wash her hands.

"How?" I ask the one word while I look at the back hallway and then back at Hailey.

"Your mom and grandmother come by at least twice a week, and she comes with them." She shrugs her shoulders and then turns to look at the television with the remote in her hand.

"All done," Mila says as she walks back into the room, kicking off her shoes and climbing on the couch. "I want to watch *Moana*."

"Mila," I say. Walking into the living room, I'm unsure of where to stand or sit. I want to run out of this house. The walls start to close in, or at least they were. The longer I stay, the looser the noose gets.

"It's fine," Hailey says from beside me. "I wanted to watch it anyway." She smiles at Mila. "Would you like some popcorn?"

"Yes," she shouts with her hands in the air like she just scored a touchdown.

"I'm going to warm up some pizza we brought. Would you like some? Would you like a beer?" Hailey walks toward the kitchen. She opens the fridge and grabs me one anyway "Here. Sit down. Relax. If it makes you feel any better, I'm just as nervous as you are." She turns away to heat me a piece of pizza, and I grab the beer from the table where she placed it. I turn and go sit down on the edge of the couch. I look forward as I take a pull from the beer, and the music from the television fills the room, along with the slam of the microwave door and the sound of plates coming down. By the time the movie is starting, Hailey comes back in with two bowls—one with chips and the other with popcorn.

"Here is your favorite bowl, Mila," she says as she hands her a pink ceramic bowl that looks like it has Mila's handprint.

"Is that her handprint?" I look over at her while she sits on the opposite couch and props her one leg up.

"Yes, we did an afternoon of ceramics." She smiles at Mila, and Mila nods her head, grabbing the popcorn and shoving it in her mouth. She doesn't say anything else because the music starts. We all turn and look at the television.

By the time half of the movie finishes, they are both sleeping on the couch. I get up to grab Mila, and her mumbling wakes Hailey. "I'm going to get going," I tell her as she blinks her eyes awake. "Thanks for having us," I tell her from over my shoulder as I walk out of the house. I get Mila in and out of her seat without waking her. Tucking her into bed, I look down at my daughter, my life, wondering what could have been.

Chapter Fourteen

Hailey

"I'm doing good," I tell my brother as I walk around the kitchen with the phone pressed between my ear and shoulder, preparing myself some toast and coffee.

"Bullshit," he counters.

"Okay fine, I'm doing better," I say as I grab the homemade jam that Delores brought me last week. For the past two weeks, it was always a surprise and pleasure when my doorbell rang. They would come with little treats, but the best was when Mila came with them because she took over the show. She is without a doubt the coolest kid I have every met. They've never brought up her mother, though, and I was not going to pry.

"Why didn't you come home this weekend?" he asks me as I hear paper rustle in the background.

"And leave my oasis? Not for all the chocolate in the world," I say, laughing, and then I hear the siren go off in the background.

"I gotta go; talk to you later," he says, disconnecting. I put the toast on a plate and grab my cup of coffee, then make my way down to the beach with the blanket draped around my neck. I place my cup on my plate as one hand whips the cover over so I can sit on it. The clouds cover the sun as the waves crash onto the shore, the white bubbles dissipating into the sand.

My mind goes back to last night when Norma came to the table. Her snide comment made me felt like the other woman again. Except for this time, I knew I was the other woman. The way that woman looked at me and judged me made my heart sink, and I knew I had to get out of there.

I place the cup and plate on the beach next to me. I hug my knees to my chest, watching birds fly through the sky, soaring high as they circle above. While enjoying the tranquility of the waves, I suddenly hear barking and giggling, causing me to look to my right. I see Mila throwing a stick, and Flounder chasing after it. Jensen walks slowly behind them carrying a cup of coffee.

"Hailey," I hear her yell as she waves her hand side to side. Her blond curls bounce as she runs over to me and her smile lights up her whole face. "Hailey," she says breathlessly when she gets to my feet. "Whatcha doing?" she asks as she stands in front of me.

"I'm just watching the water," I tell her with a smile. "What are you doing running around so early?" I ask her as Flounder comes over to me and plops down next to us, panting.

"Sorry about that." I hear Jensen's voice and look past Hailey to see that he followed her. "We didn't mean to interrupt your quiet." He takes a sip of his coffee.

"No worries. It was too quiet anyway," I tell him, looking back at Hailey. "What are your plans for today?"

"I have to go to Grandma Norma's." Turning to look at her father, she says, "I don't feel good."

"All right, so I guess we should get you into bed and take the iPad and television away so you can rest and get better," Jensen tells her, and she rolls her eyes at him.

"Fine." She huffs out, sitting down on the blanket next to me. "I feel okay. You have snacks?" She turns and looks at me, knowing full well I have her favorite snack in the house. Her question makes me throw my head back and laugh while Jensen calls her name.

"It's fine," I say, getting up and grabbing my cup and plate. "I know better than not to stock her favorites." I look back at Mila. "Would you like to come and choose?" She gets up right away and puts her hand in mine. I see Jensen's body go tight, his eyes focused on our hands.

"We don't have time," he blurts out harshly. "Mila, say goodbye."

"But Poppa," she whines, and he gives her the look that I guess means he isn't playing.

"Go on ahead; I've got to talk to Hailey," he says as she walks away with Flounder next to her. As soon as she is far enough away, he turns around and looks at me. "I don't know what game you're playing."

I cross my arms over my chest. "What game *I'm* playing?"

"All the shit with the favorite bowl to her favorite snacks," he says whispering, but his tone is anything but nice.

"You mean me being a nice person?" I glare at him. "I'm not going to apologize for liking your daughter."

"She doesn't need a mother." His words cut like a knife through my heart.

"That isn't …" I whisper, my hands now falling to my side. "That isn't what I'm doing."

"Well, I'm not going to stand by while she falls in love with you and then watch you walk away from her," he says, then turns and walks away, leaving me with my heart on my hand. Mila turns back around and waves bye to me. I wave back at her as his words sink into me.

I spend the rest of the day cleaning the house and setting up my office. His words linger in the back of my mind, and every single time I stop, it's the only thing I hear.

I sit on the swing, looking out at the water with a glass of wine as the sun falls into the horizon and the water turns black. One glass turns into two, which turns into three. Picking up the bottle and the glass, I walk down to the beach. I've never sat outside on the beach at night. I walk closer to the shore this time and sit down on the damp sand, crossing my legs as I pour another glass of wine. I look back at the house, thinking I should have left a light on.

Memories of our honeymoon flood my thoughts. The walks on the beach, just the two of us, our fingers intertwined with each other. How he'd pick up our hands and kiss my fingers. Stopping just to kiss me. *"I get to kiss you whenever I want," he used to say.*

"Fuck you, Eric," I say as a tear rolls off my chin. I try to pour another glass of wine, but it's empty.

"Why are you everywhere?" I hear from beside me, looking up to see Jensen.

"What do you want?" I ask him, turning back to look at the water. "Just keep walking and the stick up your ass might get lodged up." I mentally high five myself.

"Are you drunk?" he asks, his hands going to his hips. "Jesus, all I wanted was a nice walk on the beach."

"Then keep fucking walking." I motion with my hand down the beach. "No one is telling you to stop."

"I …" he starts and then stutters, "I'm sorry about before."

I bring my feet up to my chest. "For being a world-class asshole?" I ask him as I close my eyes and try to get the sand to stop spinning. "Which time? Because I have to say"—I laugh—"every single time I've seen you, you've been an asshole."

"Not every time," he says. And I make the mistake of looking at him. His gray sweater fits him like a glove, proving he doesn't have an ounce of fat on him, and his blue jeans hang on his hips down to his brown boots. He is so handsome ... so, so handsome.

"Go away," I say as I look back at the water, the roaring of the waves coming closer.

"It's going to be high tide soon," he tells me as he sits next to me. Bending his legs, he places his arms on his knees. "Mila's mother left her," he says softly. I turn to look at him as he turns to face me. The darkness of his eyes unreadable. "Took off and walked away without a second glance."

"My husband had two point five kids with another woman." I place my head on top of my knees as wetness soaks my jeans. "Except he didn't tell me about her."

"She left us for my best friend," he tries to counter.

"He died, leaving me alone with nothing. Nothing," I say. "His parents sent me a cease and desist letter two days before his funeral." I wipe my eyes. "I never said goodbye to him."

"She signed away her rights to Mila without a second thought and now has twin girls."

"She's a bitch," I say, and I'm not even sorry about it.

"Yeah, well, your husband isn't far off that." He looks out at the water. "I built the house for us," he starts saying, his eyes never leaving the water. "It was her surprise birthday present." I look back at the house now, hating what it stood for. "We were living in it for eight months, and it didn't come close to feeling like a home."

"It's a beautiful home," I tell him, and he nods.

"One day, she is going to regret it."

He shakes his head. "That's what I said, but then today when I walked Mila into Norma's house, there on the mantle was a picture of her with her twins." His voice trails off. "How could she love them and not our little girl?"

My hand reaches out to touch his arm. "She is the best little girl ever." He looks over at me.

"She is. She really is," I tell him as tears fall for the little girl who has captured my heart. "Luckily for Mila, she has you, and she has Heidi and Delores, and she is surrounded by love." He nods his head and returns his gaze to the water. We sit in silence as both of us fight the storm within.

He gets up, brushing his pants off. "I can see how he fell in love with you so easily." His voice soft, he says, "Good night, Hailey." He walks away, never once looking back as his body disappears into the darkness. I pick up my bottle and glass and walk to the house that holds so many bad memories for him but has saved me.

The house creaks as I settle into bed, tossing and turning, and the ticking of the clock on the wall echoes in the room. I try to shut off my brain, try counting sheep, try focusing on my breathing, but nothing works tonight. Instead, all the memories of what could have been fester.

What if I had gotten pregnant? What if I was having his baby? What if I had found out before he died? What if Mila's mother never left?

My eyes get heavy when the soft light flickers into

the room. My dreams are of the peaceful water crashing into the shore as two people try to find the answers.

Chapter Fifteen
Jensen

Is that drilling? I wonder as I open my one eye and look over at the bedside table to the empty bottle of Jack. I'm lying on my bed, dressed in exactly what I wore last night to walk on the beach. A walk on the beach to clear my thoughts. But she was there. She is everywhere now.

The whole day I felt like an asshole after basically telling her to fuck off. It's just too much. Mila being so comfortable with her just pushed me over the edge I was teetering on.

"Anyone home?" I hear Gabe yell as I groan and roll to my side. "It's almost fucking noon." I hear from my doorway. Looking over at him, I see him standing there in his workout gear.

"I thought you were gone on your weekend retreat?" I ask him as I get up from the bed. My head pounds as I walk into my bathroom and grab some aspirin.

"We got back this morning, and I needed to clear

my head," he says, and I look at him. "Don't fucking ask." He walks to the kitchen, and I hear him start the coffee. "Where is Mila?"

"Norma's," I tell him as I sit on the stool at the island, and he shakes his head.

"I know you want to be the good guy, but something about her gets under my skin." He pulls down two cups from the cabinet, then fills them with coffee and hands me mine black.

"I had to tell her to take the fucking picture of Julia and her twin girls down from the mantle." I swallow, allowing the hot coffee to burn my throat.

"Twins?" he asks, and I just nod. "Bitch," he says as he drinks his coffee.

"One big happy family." I shake my head. "Anyway. Mila is starting not to even want to go over there anymore."

"Would you?" he asks, putting his cup down. "I mean, she's a nice lady, but her daughter fucked you over, and she was still trying to tell you it wasn't what it seemed. Even after you got the divorce papers. Plus," he says as he takes another drink, "Mila gets hurt with her, and she is nowhere to be seen, yet Hailey, who"— he points at me—"is a stranger, kills herself to carry her." He drinks. "You were a big dick."

I shake my head. "If you think I was a dick then, you should have seen me yesterday when I accused her of trying to be her mother."

He stops drinking and looks at me. "You didn't."

I take a drink of hot coffee again, burning my throat.

"Oh, it gets better," I tell him. "I went for a walk later that night, and she is sitting on the beach by herself blitzed." I think of her face, the tears that stained her cheeks as she poured her heart out to me.

"Please tell me you didn't try to sleep with her while she was blitzed?" He sets his cup down hard.

"Are you insane?" My eyebrows pinch together, and he holds his hands up. "I'm not that stupid. Besides, I could never … there is just too much baggage there."

"For you or for her?" he asks, and I don't answer because the doorbell rings. I get up, going to the door, but Mila comes running in. "Poppa," she says as she jumps into my arms, and I watch Norma walk in behind her.

"Hey there, Princess," I tell her as I bring her close to me, kissing her neck. "You're home early."

"Yes," Norma says from behind her. "I'm sorry, I got an emergency call from …" And she just trails off. "I hope you don't mind."

I shake my head. "Nope." I look at my daughter. "Say goodbye to Grandma Norma."

"Bye." She waves from my arms as Norma nods her head and smiles as she walks out.

"Who just walks into a house?" Gabe asks from beside me. "Hey there, wonder woman, how is the cast?" he asks as he kisses Mila on the head.

"It's itchy," she says, "but Poppa took a stick so I can stick it in and scratch." She whispers, "It's a secret." And we all laugh.

"I won't tell anyone," Gabe says as he walks to the

door. "I have to get ready for this Sunday dinner. You coming?" he asks as he walks backward, and I nod. "Good. See you there." He turns and slams the door.

"So what did you do at Grandma Norma's house?" I ask her as I put her down and pick up her backpack that she dropped when she ran to me.

"We did a mani-pedi, but she didn't want to paint my nails pink," she says as she goes to the cabinet, grabbing her stool to get something to eat. "Can I watch *The Boss Baby*?" she asks as she bounces to the couch and turns on the television.

"Sure," I say as I grab my coffee and go sit with her. "You need to take a bath before we go to GG Delores's," I tell her. She hums okay as she eats a rice crispy treat and we watch *The Boss Baby*. My head finally stops throbbing, and we change before leaving.

"I look like a princess," she says as she puts on her pink dress. Spinning on one foot, she watches the dress float around her legs.

"Yes, you do," I say, grabbing my wallet from the counter and putting it in the back pocket of my jeans. "Let's go," I say as she puts on her silver glitter shoes that my mother bought her last year for Thanksgiving. I slide on my aviator glasses as we walk out.

We pull up to Delores's house, and I have to park at the end of the driveway. "I guess she invited everyone in town," I say as I open the door and wait for Mila to unbuckle herself. I grab a sweater for her along with her backpack that holds her pjs.

As we walk up to the house, we hear voices from

inside. I open the door and see people from the senior center. I walk through the house, stopping to say hi when I know someone, and head outside to see tables set up everywhere. I look around for my mother or my grandmother, but my eyes stop the minute I see soft blond hair. She's standing next to Crystal dressed in black jeans, torn at the knee and tight, showing off her lean legs. A white cotton shirt tucked in on one side while the other side hangs down. She's wearing a light green button-down shirt on top, rolled up at the wrists. She smiles at something Crystal says, and I realize the pain from last night is gone. Or she is really good at hiding it. She turns her head as if she senses me staring at her, her eyes finding mine. She smiles shyly, looking back down at the glass of wine in her hand.

"Finally." I feel a hand slap my back and turn to see Brody with Darla right next to him, holding his hand. "Oh, I think I see a princess," he says to Mila as she smiles and spins in her dress for him.

"Have you seen my mom?" I ask them, and they both point to the side where she stands talking to Luigi. "I'm going to go see Grandma," I tell Mila who has walked over to Darla to play with her bracelets and asks to wear some.

"I got her," Brody says as I make my way through people who stop to say hello to me. By the time I get to my mother, she is sitting at a table with my grand-mother.

"You look so handsome," my mother says. I smile at her as my grandmother sits back in her chair. "Where is Mila?" she asks as we look around the yard and find her in Hailey's arms. Mila's playing with Hailey's necklace as they talk.

"Isn't she stunning?" my grandmother says, and I don't answer her because I'm not sure who she is talking about. "Her grandmother didn't think she would ever get over what she went through. But every day, I see her slowly crawling her way back up." My eyes never leave the sight before me. Mila points over to me, and I smile and raise my hand in hello. She places Mila on her feet, and Mila makes her way over to me. Hailey watches till she gets to me and then turns around to walk away as Mila climbs into my lap.

"Grandma, when are we going to eat?" She looks at them. "If we don't eat soon, I'm going to need a snack." We all laugh at her as the waiters start setting up the food for the buffet-style meal.

"I love having these Sunday dinners just because," my grandmother says. "It brings the community together and gets people out. Gets other people to socialize," she says as she raises her chin. I look in the direction she is looking and see Garrett, the owner of the local pub, talking to Hailey. They laugh about something, and she tucks her hair behind her ear, showing her long neck. I don't listen to the chatter around me; I just look around, but my eyes always go back to Hailey, the pull stronger than I can resist.

"Let's eat," I tell Mila. I get up, and we walk hand in hand to the buffet. I walk over as I stand in line, grabbing two plates and piling food on them. "Where do you want to sit?" I ask her as Brody calls my name. I look up and see him sitting with Darla, who is having a conversation with Hailey as they both eat. I walk over to the table with Mila following me. "Grab a seat, Mila." At the sound of my voice, Hailey's head pops up.

"I want to sit on this chair." She grabs the chair right next to Hailey and puts her knee on the chair to climb up. She sits on her knees, so she can see the table, and I set her plate in front of her.

"I wonder if there is a booster seat anywhere?" I ask, looking around. A chair in front of me moves, and Crystal sits down, followed by the chair next to her moving as Gabe sits down.

I look to my right at Gabe. "Watch her," I say, gesturing to Mila, who is grabbing her fork to eat some noodles.

I walk inside to grab her booster chair and walk out just as Hailey is tucking a napkin into the top of her dress.

"Look, Poppa, to keep me clean," she says as her hands touch her chest, leaving sauce on it.

"Good idea," I say as I pick her up and place the booster on the chair and then set her on it. "Better?" I ask. She nods and then starts eating again. The meal talk stays neutral as Darla asks Hailey about her business of creating websites. Hailey answers all her questions and gives her suggestions on how to grow her salon. As the sun sets, the lights around the yard illuminate. The plates are cleared, and Mila sits on my lap watching something on my phone.

Crystal gets up to get coffee, and Hailey gets up with her. "Does anyone want anything?" she asks the table, looking around. Mila looks up.

"Can I get some cake?" Mila asks me, and I nod. "I'm coming," she says as she climbs down from my lap and grabs Crystal's and Hailey's hands. They both look down and smile at her. I watch them walk away discussing all the pie they want to eat.

"Why were they invited?" Gabe asks from beside me. I look at him, and he turns his head back from them to us.

"I'm going to go out on a limb here," Darla says, "and say that someone has gotten under your skin." She points at Gabe.

"Please." He rolls his eyes but doesn't say anything else because his gaze rolls back to the two girls.

"I don't know if you know this, but Crystal is the talk of the salon. Ever since Mrs. Peterson broke her hip and she took care of her, she is the light of everyone's talk."

"I'm the one who operated on her, not my nurse."

"Oh, someone is sensitive," Brody says as he takes a pull from his beer bottle.

"Fuck you." He throws his napkin down and gets up. "I'm out." I watch him walk around people till he walks around the house to where his car must be parked.

"I brought you cherry pie," Mila says as she carries spoons in her hands, and Crystal and Hailey each carry two plates.

"Here you go," Hailey says as she places the cherry pie in front of me and places the blueberry in front of Mila. She grabs her own plate, filled with apple pie, from Crystal, and Crystal places her key lime pie down in front of her. "We couldn't carry any coffee," she tells the table as Mila hands her a spoon, and she smiles at her.

"That looks so good," Darla says from beside her as Hailey offers her a clean spoon and her plate.

"I want to taste too," Mila says as Hailey puts the apple pie next to her so she can get a piece, mixing her blueberry spoon with her apple. "That one is good too," she says as she finishes her bite but goes back to her blueberry.

"Okay," Darla says, "it's time for us to hit the road." She looks over at Brody, who smiles at her as he gets up and grabs her hand. She says goodbye to us, then kisses Mila.

"Do you guys mind giving me a ride?" Crystal asks as Hailey looks over at her. "I'm beat from this weekend. Camping is not team building," she says. "Let's just say you're lucky we all came back because my vote was to toss Gabe out."

"I'm done," Hailey says from her side and starts to rise.

"No, stay, you never get out. Mingle with the single," she says as she points her head in the direction of Garrett. The pie suddenly tastes bitter in my mouth, but Hailey just shakes her head as Crystal leaves.

We don't say anything as Mila finishes her pie and then gets down to go in search of water. "This was nice," Hailey says from the side, and I look over at her. She really is stunning without a stitch of makeup on, and looking at her, I see little freckles on her nose.

"Um, I want to say sorry about last night." I sit up and place my hands on the table and look over at her.

"I was hoping I had imagined that conversation," she says softly. "I don't usually blurt out my feelings."

"You know what they say." I take my beer, pulling in some. "A drunken man's words are a sober man's thoughts."

She taps her finger on the table in front of her. "Is that right? Well, I did call you an asshole, so that would be correct."

"About that," I start, looking around for Mila who is now sitting with my mother as she rocks her. "I would really like to start over."

"Which time?" She pushes the plates from in front of her as she leans on the table. "Which time do you want to take back?" she asks as I look into her eyes. The sadness from yesterday replaced by a soft light.

"Every single time." And ain't that the truth.

She nods her head and looks down, no doubt calling me an asshole in her mind, but she turns to look at me and holds out her hand. "I'm Hailey."

Her hand's stretched out as a peace offering. I look at it, and I see she wears no rings. I lean over and take her hand in mine, the heat from my hand warming her cold, delicate one. "I'm Jensen or, as people call me,

Walker." She smiles. I don't let her hand go, and we just keep shaking it up and down. "And I believe I owe you an apology and a thank you."

"Do you?" she asks confused. "For what?"

"I'm sorry for being an asshole to you." I start and let her hand go to fall to her side. "I shouldn't have taken it out of you. For that, I'm genuinely sorry. And …" I'm about to continue when my mother approaches the table with a sleeping Mila.

"She is out for the night, I think," she says as she glances at Mila's head on her shoulder.

"I should go," Hailey says as she gets up, and I grab Mila from my mom.

"I'm going to go also. We can walk out together," I tell my mother as I place Mila on my chest. My mother kisses my cheek and gives Hailey a hug as we walk out. When she stops at her car, I speak. "I never finished what I had to say." She looks up as she opens her car door, surprised I'm bringing it up again. "Thank you for putting my little girl before yourself." I look over at her little cast, that is literally indestructible.

She reaches out and pushes Mila's hair away from her face. "For her, anything," she says, smiling. "Have a great night, Jensen." She ducks and gets in her car as I continue to mine, the night playing over and over in my head long after I've fallen asleep.

Chapter Sixteen
Hailey

"Look at this," I say as I open the screen door and see Mila standing with Delores and Heidi. "Isn't it my three favorite girls?" I say as Mila walks in and takes off her shoes.

"We brought pie," she says as she unzips her jacket and takes it off. "Blueberry." She puts her jacket on the chair near the door, and continues inside.

"Did you? It's a good thing because I'm really hungry," I tell her as Delores and Heidi walk in. "Mila, look at the basket next to the fireplace." I point at the pink basket I picked up this week when I made the roadtrip to Walmart. I picked up coloring books, crayons, and little stamps to keep her busy while I chat with her two grandmothers.

"Look at all this," she says as she lifts the basket to the table and begins taking things out. "Is it all for me?"

"Who else would it be for?" I tell her as I walk over.

"Why don't you color a picture while we have coffee?" She nods her head and flips to the page she wants to color. I get up, going to the kitchen. "Okay, you two. We need to talk." I fold my arms so they know I mean business. They look at each other and then at me. "Now, you know I love you guys, and I love, love, love the visits," I tell them as Heidi goes to put the coffee on, looking back at me.

"I actually look forward to it more than you know," she says, and I nod.

"But, and this is a big but." I look at them. "I will not be in the middle of Jensen and you guys."

They both look at each other. "The other night, he was surprised Mila came here, let alone all the things we've done."

"Jensen came here?" Heidi says.

"Don't change the subject." I point at her. "He brought me home because my foot was throbbing, and I didn't have my car. Now" I say, looking down, "I've come to love that little girl, but I will not have her here without her father's consent." I wipe the tear away, my stomach hurting at the thought of not seeing her again. Delores walks to me and holds my arms.

"Okay," she says softly. "We never meant any harm."

"I know," I say, "but I was just put in an awkward position, and it didn't help that he was blindsided." I look over at Heidi who is on the phone.

"Walker, we are taking Mila to bring Hailey pie," she starts saying. "Call me when you get this." I shake my head and laugh at these two.

"You don't play fair." I point at Heidi.

"Why are you crying?" I hear Mila from the living room.

"I'm not crying," I tell her, "I just got something in my eye."

"That happened to Poppa to when he watched *The Little Mermaid* and she went to live with people," Mila says as she looks down at her picture, coloring as we laugh at her.

"Now," Delores says, "we are actually here for business." She sits down. "The summer fair is coming up soon, and we thought we could do one of those web thingies."

"A website?" I ask them as I sit down and cut the pie and serve myself a piece. "Mila, honey, you want some pie?" I ask over my shoulder. She brings her stuff to the table and climbs on the chair next to me, putting her book beside her.

"So what is this summer fair?" I ask them as they fill me in on this street festival that takes place right around Independence Day; there's a farmers market, as well as pony rides, and local artists come out. It sounds amazing. "Okay, so how about you guys bring me some pictures that I can work with and I will put something together?"

"How much will it be?" Heidi asks as she takes a piece of pie.

"Nothing," I tell them as I take a bite of my pie and smile at them.

"You can't do it for free."

I sit up and take a deep breath. "You guys gave me life again." I look back down and then up again. "I thought I wasn't going to survive. And then I came here, and you guys gave me back me. I could never repay you," I tell them as they both look at me speech-less. Nothing needs to be said. They don't visit for much longer and promise to send me the pictures for the website. I continue my work for the day, not look-ing up until almost seven.

Crystal comes in drained from work, grabbing a piece of pie and going up to her room. I make myself something quick and grab my laptop to eat outside on the swing, flipping through my emails and planning my day. I close it down and get up, making my way down to the beach. I love being so close to it, love that I get to breathe the salty air all the time. I wrap the knitted sweater around me and sit down, letting my mind clear.

It started as my therapy to purge Eric from my sys-tem, but now it's more about finding out what I want for me. A dog barking makes me look down the beach. He runs to me, this time coming in to lick my face. "Flounder." I push him away as he sits beside me, and I see Jensen walk toward me. His blue jeans torn at the thigh, his caramel-color sweater casual with a red t-shirt sticking out a bit from the bottom. His scruff still present as he walks to me smiling. He is so handsome, and he doesn't even realize it.

"Shocking meeting you here," he says as I look up and smile at his joke. "Mind if I join you?" I turn my wrist, my hand gesturing for him to have a seat.

"Where is Mila?" I ask as he looks at me. "Spending the night at Nana's house. It's her paint night, and Mila somehow convinced them she should be there."

I laugh at the thought. "She is going to make a great lawyer one day." I look at Flounder who sits right by our feet. "So how was your day?"

He nods his head. "It was good, busy. Spring is always a busy time. People coming out of hibernation. People changing things. People wanting a new house." He puts his hand behind him and leans back, stretching out his legs. "What about you?"

"I finally got my email count down to zero." I put my hands up in a cheering motion. "I took about a month off when Eric died, or maybe more, I don't really remember much, but it feels good to get back."

"How long were you married?" he asks.

"Six months, twenty-one days." I smirk as he raises his eyebrows. "Not that I was counting. What about you?"

"Julia and I were together since we were high school." He looks at the water. "Isn't that a cliché?"

I cross my legs. "Yes, but everyone has the dream to marry her high school sweetheart." I smile.

"Then cheat on him," he counters, laughing.

"Not the cheating part. Not everyone cheats." I look at my fingers then look up. "So can I ask you a question?"

He looks at me confused. "That is a loaded question."

"When did you wake up and not have the pain?"

"I can't pinpoint it, but I think it's still there, just lingering in the back. In the beginning, I would wake up every day with hatred for her, but then still long for her to come back."

"Yeah, I'm at that stage now," I tell him. "Lately, though, I don't even want him to come back. I just want him gone, out of my mind."

He laughs at me. "I burned all of Julia's pictures," he tells me. "Every single one of them. Except one." He doesn't say which one, and I don't ask.

"When did you start dating again?" I think about the question and about how it's not a question he needs to answer.

"Hailey, I live in a small town. A town that if I walked down the street with someone, it would probably be the town gossip for the month. I don't date."

I look at him in shock. "You don't date?"

"Are you just talking about sex?" He laughs as he looks at me.

My mouth opens and closes. "Um …"

"Because if your asking that …" he starts, and I hold up my hand.

"NO," I yell as I jump to my feet.

His hand comes out, and he grabs my hand, bringing me back down next to him. "Sit down." He laughs as his hand still holds mine as sand gets between us.

"I don't want to know that," I say, pulling my hand away from his and brushing off the sand.

"There isn't a set time for you to feel like yourself.

There isn't a right or wrong time for you to want to date. No one knows but you."

I nod my head, thinking about what he is saying. "Thank you," I tell him as I put my hands behind me and lean back, "for letting me stay in your house even though you hate it."

"In all fairness, I had no choice." He looks over as he leans back on his hands again, the heat of his hand so close to mine I feel it. "But you're welcome." I laugh at his words because it couldn't be more right; no one gave him a chance to say no.

"Favorite food?" I ask him, switching it up.

"Ribs, chicken, steak," he answers without thinking about it.

"So a meat guy?" I joke. "I almost gave up meat my senior year of high school," I tell him, and he covers his mouth with his hand in shock. "I know. Trust me, I know. I just couldn't go the final step." I laugh.

"Favorite movie?" he asks.

"*Sixteen Candles*," I say, and he groans.

"You know that Jake Ryan dude is a carpenter now, right?" he tells me.

"He is so hot. I bet he could do lots with his hands." I wink at him as he pulls his knees up and hangs his hands on them.

We spend the next hour talking about everything and nothing. At the end of the night, I didn't want him to leave nor did I get the feeling he wanted to leave either. He gets up on his feet and holds out a hand to help me stand. Flounder looks over his shoulder from his spot on the sand. "This was nice," I tell him.

He puts his hands in his back pockets, the sweater pulling across his chest, and he smiles. "It was a good evening."

He smiles and looks down and then up at me, or down at me since he's that much taller. "Go on up." He motions to the house with his head.

"You going soft on me, Jensen?" I laugh as I start to walk to the house then turn. "You aren't that scary, you know?" I turn back and run to the house as his laughter fills the night. I walk in and shut off the lights, but don't leave till I see him walk away. Holding his head high, he walks down the beach with his hands in his pockets.

"Late night visitor?" Crystal says from behind me, causing me to jump and yelp.

"You scared the shit out of me," I tell her as she leans on the doorjamb with a coffee cup in her hand. She smirks at me.

"So your visitor?" she asks as she looks at me.

"You want to do this? What about the hickey on your left boob?" I point at her as her eyes go to slits.

"I don't know what you're talking about." She feigns ignorance.

"Really? So who is the guy?" I ask her, and she just shrugs her shoulders.

"Again, you're changing the subject," she points out to me.

"So are you," I tell her as she turns and walks away. "Night, hooker." She flips me the bird as she walks away.

My dreams that night aren't of the storm brewing but of calm waters with the sun shining.

Chapter Seventeen

Jensen

I lock the back door as I walk through the house, going straight to my room. The phone in my pocket buzzes, so I take it out and see a shit ton of missed calls, some from Gabe, some from Brody, and one from my mom.

I open the text message from Gabe.

There is this bowling shit this Friday. Are you in?

Why haven't you gotten back to me?

Where the fuck are you?

OMG ARE YOU WITH A GIRL? YOUR HAND MIGHT GET JEALOUS!

I laugh at the last one and send him the finger emoji.

Then my phone lights up with his name.

"Where the fuck were you?" he asks as I hear Sports Center in the back ground.

"I went for a walk on the beach. Mom has Mila," I tell him, taking off my shirt.

"So are you in for this bowling shit? I asked Brody, and he said he would."

What are you talking about?" I ask him, kicking off my shoes.

"This weekend at that retreat, they said we should have office gatherings, and someone mentioned bowling," he says as he sighs. "So if I have to suffer, I'm bringing my people in."

I laugh at him. "Okay, I'll talk to Mom about babysitting Mila."

"Good, and who knows, maybe you might meet someone."

"Thanks," I tell him as Hailey's face flashes through my mind, "but I'm okay."

"Whatever, dude. If your hand keeps you that warm, I don't want to break up a happy home."

"Fuck you," I tell him. Hanging up, I bring up the other texts. My mother sent me a painting of Mila, and I swear it looks like a dick with balls, but it's a pink spaceship.

I also text asking if she can babysit for me, and she calls me back. What is up with people and texting today?

"Hey, honey," she says as soon as I answer. "Mila is sleeping."

"Okay? Was everything okay tonight?" I ask as she tells me about the night, but the only think I can think of is my walk on the beach.

"So can you watch Mila on Friday?" I ask her.

"Actually, I was going to ask if I could take her away for the weekend?"

"Where are you going?"

"My friend and I are going up to the springs for the weekend of hiking, and we will be stopping at Eleanor's ranch."

"Oh yeah, she'll love that," I tell her as we finish the conversation. She promises to bring Mila home sometime tomorrow. When I finally fall into bed shortly after, my dreams are of the beach, the sun, and blond hair running in the distance.

The next morning, I decided to take a walk on the beach. Bringing Flounder's ball, I throw it and he chases it. I walk by the house with the drapes still closed, wondering if she's sleeping, wondering if she had any more nightmares about her dick head ex. I shake my head, thinking how stupid he could have been.

For the whole day, the conversation I had with Hailey last night played on my mind. The question of getting over the bad. I let it all fester inside me. Let it simmer, letting me work through my own thoughts.

I'm thinking of her the whole time I take a shower on that Friday night; the whole time I touch myself in the shower, it's her eyes I envision. I get out, planning to see her tonight, even if I have to sit outside the house on the beach. I grab my light blue jeans and white dress shirt, slipping my black V-neck sweater over it. Running my hands through my hair, I put on my black boots, then grab my wallet and keys and make my way to the bowling alley.

I look down at my phone after I park and find a couple of missed texts from Brody.

Telling me to hurry my ass up.

I walk in and wave at a couple of people I know when I turn, colliding with Hailey. Her scent of flowers invades me. "Hey," I say as I grab her to make sure I don't knock her over.

"Hey, yourself," she says as she steadies herself, and I take in her fucking outfit. It's just jeans, but they have tears all down the front, and they are tight and mold to her. Her big knitted sweater goes down in a V, till just above her tits, where she has some lace shit on under it. "Are you here with someone?" she asks as she holds her bowling shoes in her hand. My stomach falls as I think she might be on a fucking date.

"I'm meeting Gabe and his gang," I say as I put my hands in my pockets, the feeling of her sweater still on my fingers.

"Oh good, so I know at least one person," she says with a smile, and I take in her single braid on one side. My fingers itch to touch her neck.

"Yeah, are you here with Crystal?" I ask her as I walk over to the counter and get my shoes.

"Yeah, I was, but then I looked around, and I can't find her." She continues looking around. "I guess she must be in the bathroom." I follow her as she leads me to a group of about twenty people. Most I know from the clinic, but some are new faces. I look around to see if Brody is anywhere close. "I guess we are on the same team," she says from beside me as I look up and see that there are six on our team.

"Is it just the two of us?" I ask but then turn to see Brody and Darla walk from the bar carrying a tray of beers. "Hey." I jerk my chin up to him as I go grab the tray from Darla.

"Thank you, sugar." She smiles at me as she walks over to Hailey. "I love your shirt," she says as she takes in Hailey.

"Whoa." I hear Brody next to me as he watches me watch Hailey. "You might want to simmer down there, big boy. You keep looking at her like she's your next meal, and she is going to get creeped out." He laughs as he puts down the tray of beer and kisses Hailey's cheek. Why the fuck is he kissing her cheek?

"There you are." I hear Hailey say from beside me, and I look up to see Crystal coming down from the doorway.

"Sorry, I forgot something in the car," she says as she grabs her shoes.

Hailey laughs next to her. "That's funny; we didn't drive my car here." Crystal looks like a deer in head-lights. I look over at the door as Gabe walks in. His shirt buttoned all wrong and wiping his lips with his thumb.

He looks up at me as I look to see if anyone else saw, and I'm not surprised to find Hailey looking at him and then back at Crystal. She looks over at me, and her eyes go big. I shake my head, and she nods. I meet him halfway.

"You are fucking Crystal? Are you insane?"

"Hey," he says, pointing at me, "I'm not fucking anyone."

"Really?" I tilt my head, looking at him. "You still

have lip gloss on your lips, and your shirt is not but-toned properly."

"Fuck," he says as he walks away to the bathroom. I head back over to the group.

"So," I say, sitting next to Hailey. "Who is going to go first?"

I stretch my arms out on both sides. Darla jumps to her feet.

"I'll go first," she says as she gives Brody a kiss, and I look over to see Crystal socializing with the other nurses.

"So are we going to discuss what we just saw?" Hailey leans in to me, her shoulder fitting against me perfectly. "Did you know?"

I look over at her, seeing the sparkle in her eye. "No, did you?" I ask her quietly with a smile. She shakes her head.

"Hailey," Brody says loudly, and she jumps away from me. "Your turn."

She taps my legs as she gets up. "Be right back," she says as she gets up. Going to the balls, she grabs a pink ball and looks over at the other lane. I've seen the guy at the clinic a couple of times. He tells her something, and she throws her head back and laughs. She watches him bowl, and then he comes over as if tell her what to do, and she does and knocks down eight pins. She squeals and then walks back over and high fives him.

"Who the fuck is that?" I ask Gabe as I point at the guy.

"Don't fucking touch my pediatrician. He just started. He's the best around," Gabe says as he looks over at the rest of his staff, seeing Crystal talk to someone I've never seen before.

His teeth clench as I slap his back. "Relax, dude, it's nothing." I look up and see it's my turn, so I walk up to Hailey and her friend. "Hey, nice to meet you, I'm Walker."

I put my hand out as I put my other hand on Hailey's back while the guy reaches forward. "I'm Alan. Do you work at the clinic?"

I laugh as I pull my hand back. "Nope. I own Walker Construction next door."

"Oh," he says, pointing, "you guys are building my house."

"Really?" I say, not surprised. "Well, let me know if you need anything. If you'll excuse me, it's my turn." I turn to Hailey. "I think Crystal was looking for you." I point back at the seats to see Crystal is actually there.

"Well, see you later, Alan." Hailey smiles and walks back while I grab a ball and bowl a strike. "Look at you, professional bowler and all," she says as she drinks a glass of beer.

"I'm a man of many talents," I tell her as Crystal pretends to vomit in her mouth.

"Really? So besides bowling and being a pretty cool dad, what other talents do you have?" She crosses her hands over her chest as she smiles, and I want to bury my hand in her hair and kiss that smile off her lips.

"I can cook a mean steak," I tell her as I put my hands in my back pockets before I do something she isn't ready for.

"Is that so?" She laughs as she has another drink of beer. "You'll have to show me one day," she says as Crystal shrieks and jumps up down after getting a strike. She points to Gabe and flips him the bird.

"Soft, my ass," she says as she comes back and sits next to him. "I believe it's your turn. Loser buys the winner lunch for a week." She smiles as he glares at her. "Should I just give you my orders now?"

"It isn't over till the tenth frame, doll face," Gabe tells her.

"Ewww, did you just call me doll face?" Her face in a grimace. "I mean, it's better than pain in my ass." She shrugs.

"You are a pain in my ass. For once, I'd like to have a day when you don't second-guess everything I do," he says as he looks back to grab his ball and she yells.

"For once, I'd like to go to work with a doctor who I don't have to second-guess. If you want, I can transfer to pediatrics. Alan likes me," she tells him as she leans back and smiles at Alan who waves. I look at Gabe and think he's going to throw the bowling ball at him. "Let's see what you can do, Doctor," Crystal says as he bowls a strike and turns around with his hands over his head.

"You two do realize that this is ten frames, and we just did only one," Brody says as he grabs Darla to sit on his lap.

"Please. I've got him beat; he's a princess," Crystal says as she gulps down some beer.

"Princess?" Gabe says as he laughs. "You cried when I picked up a frog and showed it to you."

Crystal slams down her hands. "That fucker was going to jump at me." She storms up. "I want to change teams."

We all laugh at them. "Too late," he says as he looks at the screen. "Darla, you're up." Crystal glares at him as I sit down and watch. Hailey looks around, and when she sees me sitting down, she comes over.

"I don't think those two are going to be able to work and have sex without killing each other." Hailey crosses her legs and leans in to whisper in my ear. I turn to look at her and see the sparkle again.

"You're beautiful when you smile." The words slip out before I can stop them. She looks down and then up again.

"So when are you going to make me steak?" she asks as she drinks some more beer. I notice it's her second one. Liquid courage.

"Tell you what, I'll cook the steaks tomorrow night, but you have to come over and help me." My hands itch to touch her as I rub my thighs.

"Hooker," Crystal yells back, and Hailey jumps up.

The rest of the evening, we mingle and laugh. Brody ends up winning the game. Crystal beats Gabe by one point.

"The machine is broken," he said as he looked at the score. "There has to be a glitch in the system. I had one more strike than you did."

Crystal looks at her nails and then up again. "Yes,

and then you knocked two pins down, which means you suck and I win so … I'll text you my orders."

The rest of the clinic people come over and discuss hitting up the bar. Crystal looks at Hailey. "You go ahead. I'm going to head home," Hailey says as she looks around.

"Walker"—Crystal looks at me—"you going home? Can you drive her?"

"I'm not going to the bar," Alan says with a smile.

"I got her, but thanks." I look at him as we say bye to everyone else and walk out. I open her door for her as she giggles, and I shake my head. She is half blitzed.

I start the car, and the song "Don't You Wanna Stay" comes on, and she buckles her seat belt. "I love this song," she says as she sings off-key. I look out the window as I drive up to the house, the lights outside lit up. She unbuckles her seat belt. "Will you come sit with me?" she asks, and at that moment, I'm going to give her whatever she wants as long as she keeps the sparkle in her eyes.

I put the car in park, then make my way out of the car as she meets me and opens her hand. "Let's sit by the water," she says, and I put my hand in hers, and we walk down to the water.

We sit down in our normal spots, gazing out at the water. "Did you really mean you're cooking for me tomorrow?" She looks over at me as she unties the braid in her hair and it now falls over her.

"I never joke about steak," I tell her as she smiles and then looks forward.

"I had a lot of fun tonight," she says. She turns around and faces my side, crossing her legs as her bent knees rest on top of mine. "Like a lot, a lot of fun," she says, tucking her hair behind her ears.

"Did you? What was it that made it so much fun?" I put my hand on her knee as I ask her the question.

"Just being out there with other people and not feel-ing sad." She gets up and spins. "Do you have your phone with you?" She looks down as I hand her my phone and she plays a song I don't recognize. She holds the phone in one hand while she holds out her other hand. "Will you dance with me?"

I grab her hand as I get up. Wrapping an arm around her waist, I hold her hand with the phone with the other while she puts one hand on my shoulder. We move in a circle on the sand as the lyrics play. "Are you going to kiss me or not?" As my gaze snaps up and I look in her eyes, they sparkle even in the dark.

"How drunk are you right now?" I ask her as she stops dancing.

"Drunk enough to ask you"—she looks down and then up again—"and sober enough to hope you kiss me." My hands drop from her, and I move her hair away from her face as the wind blows.

My hands cup her face as her smile never wavers, the song blaring from my phone that now lays in the sand. "All night I had to hide my hands from grabbing you, they itched to touch you." I bring her face closer to mine.

"So"—she licks her lips—"are you gonna kiss me or not?" She laughs, and my lips crash into hers.

Chapter Eighteen
Hailey

I'm free, or at least I feel free. Sitting on the cold sand, I feel my head turning a bit. My heart is fluttering, my hands are clammy, and I have a smile on my face that seems to be permanent. This whole night was so different. Sitting without a care in the world. Being embraced by people and not judged or looked at differently. It was everything.

But then I looked into Jensen's light brown eyes, and I got lost. Lost in him, lost in the feel of him, lost in myself. Every time he touched me, my body would tingle. I would feel his touch long after his hand was gone.

I sat in the car with him, so close, and knew I didn't want the night to end. Knew that, if I let him go, I would regret it. Now, I'm standing here on the beach that let me become whole again, on the beach that didn't give me answers but let me make peace. On the beach that made me want to wake up the next day. Asking him to kiss me, I looked into his eyes for the answers for anything. His hands push my hair back while it blows in the soft wind as I smile at him.

"How drunk are you right now?" He asks me the question, and I stop moving, thinking of how I want to answer.

"Drunk enough to ask you," I answer him honestly as I look down at our bodies pushed together and then up again, "and sober enough to hope you kiss me." His hands drop from my waist as my heart beats louder than the music playing on his phone.

His warm hands come up to cup my face as my heart beat continues faster and faster, and my stomach fills with little butterflies. But one thing never goes away, and it's the smile on my face. "All night …" He starts talking, and his thumbs gently move over my face. "I had to hide my hands from grabbing you because they itched to touch you." He brings my face closer to his, so close I can feel his breath on me and goose bumps cover my body. Not because I'm cold, but because I'm that much closer to him. The anticipation of his lips on mine has me licking my lips.

"So," I ask him as the song plays, "are you gonna kiss me or not?" A nervous laugh escapes me, but it dies as soon as his lips touch mine. My hands go to his waist, pulling him closer. He tilts his head to the side, and I sigh when he slides his tongue into my mouth, and I revel in him. The taste of him and beer. His hands slide from my cheeks to my hair, and he grabs it in his fist. My hands go to his face, my fingers rubbing through the scruff of his face, bringing his face closer to me. My body wakes up as I press myself into him. Our mouths never leave each other as our hands roam. Mine go from his face to his hair and his go from my hair to my back and then down to my waist. As he breaks the kiss with a small peck, he looks at me. My hands go back down to his face, and my fingers trace his lips, my fingers tingling.

"Are you okay?" he asks as his eyes search mine, and his hands rub up my back to my hair. "Um …" he says as he looks down at my lips. I lean in and kiss him this time. I'm the one placing my lips on his, showing him I'm okay. That I'm more than okay. The only sound around us is the crashing of the waves and now a ringing cell phone. I pull back and look down at our feet to see that Gabe is calling.

"Fuck," he says as he bends down and picks up the phone. "This better be you dying," he says. I move into him and he wraps one hand around my waist. "Yeah, yeah," I hear him say. "I'm on my way," he says as he hangs up the phone, placing it in his back pocket. "Gabe's car got vandalized." I look at him in shock. "I have to go get him," he says. I nod my head, and we turn to walk toward his car, his hand grabbing mine. I stand by the front door as I look at him, and he looks at me. His hand leaves mine so he can touch my face. "So tomorrow?" he asks as he smiles, and I lean in to kiss him.

"Tomorrow." I kiss him, my lips on his as I breathe out a contented sigh. "Be careful," I tell him as he gets in his truck and rolls the window down. "Get inside, Hailey," he says. I watch him pull around until his red lights are in the distance. I walk back inside, locking the door but keeping the outside lights on for Crystal. I walk to the living room and turn on a dim light for her in there also. When I fall into my bed, my hands still smell of Jensen as I trace my tingling lips. I turn to look outside and replay the kiss over and over again as I drift off.

When my eyes open the next day, I'm still wearing a smile. Getting up and heading out to make coffee, I stop when I see Crystal walking in. "Did you leave to go out for doughnuts or is this your walk of shame?" I ask her as I walk to the machine and start the coffee.

"I don't want to discuss it," she says as plops down at the table and places her head on it. "I'm going to sleep till Monday."

I take down two coffee cups, then fill them and carry them to the table. I sit with my feet up on the chair and tie my hair on the top of my head. "I kissed Jensen last night," I tell her as I hide the smile with the coffee cup, but you can't hide the emotions from my eyes. Crystal raises her head from the table.

"With tongue?" I nod my head like a badass. "HUSSY," she yells, and she slaps the table. "And how was it?"

I try to think of how to describe how I felt when he kissed me, what I felt after, what it all meant, and the only thing that I could come up with was, "Perfect." I say, smiling, "Absolutely perfect."

"I thought he was going to knock the shit out of Alan and bowl with his head. Every single time." She laughs as she takes a sip of coffee. "It was quite funny. Gabe and I had a side bet going."

"You and Gabe have a lot going," I counter and see her eyes get glossy. "I know you're a big girl, but I just want you to be careful. I mean, he's your boss."

"Technically, his father is my boss, but it was a one-time thing," she points out, but I glare at her. "Okay, fine, it was more than a one-time thing, but it's done." She puts her hands up. "No blood, no foul, or whatever the country folks say."

"I think it's no harm, no foul, country or not," I say as I sit up. "I just don't want you to get hurt." I look at her.

"Hailey, it's fine." She looks down and then up. "I promise I'm okay." She gets up, grabs her cup of coffee, and walks up the stairs. My phone starts ringing from somewhere in the house. I run to my room to where I think the ringing is coming from and then it stops.

"Fuck," I say as I toss the covers up and down, looking under the pillow and finally finding it there. I see I have a missed call from an unknown caller. I'm about to put the phone down when I see I have an email alert from a J. Walker. I slide my finger across the M logo and open it up.

Hey, I guess I'm really out of the loop because I forgot to get your number, and I don't even know if you check your emails on the weekend.

Here is my number.

I don't bother reading the rest of it. Instead, I click the number and press call.

He answers on the first ring. "Hello." The sound of his voice makes me smile, and the butterflies start in my stomach.

"Jensen," I say, "it's Hailey."

He laughs. "Look outside," he says as I walk to the back door and see him standing by the beach with Flounder next to him.

"I'll be right out." I look down at my charcoal sleep pants tight around the ankles with the string tied at the waist and a white t-shirt. I grab the long knit black sweater to wrap around me and slide into my Uggs. I walk down, putting my hand in front of my eyes to block the sun as Flounder comes to me and nudges my leg. I pet his head and look up and Jensen is there. "Morning." I smile at him. He's wearing his work gear. "Have you been out here long?"

"No." He shrugs, looking down then up again. "Maybe an hour."

I clap my hand together, laughing. "Why didn't you come knock on my door?"

"I didn't know if you were up or not," he says as I step up to him. His hand goes to my face, and he takes my lips in a kiss that starts off soft but quickly heats up. His hands slide under the sweater to my waist, leaving me breathless as he kisses me gently. "I could get used to kissing you every morning."

I smile as I wrap my arms around his waist and pull

him closer. "I don't think I would complain," I say as he holds me.

"Are we still on for dinner?" he asks as I tilt my head back and smile.

"I really hope so," I tell him as he kisses me again.

"Okay, good. Now I can go to work." He smiles as he rubs my arms. "How about you come by at around five?"

"Sounds like a plan." I let my arms fall from him. "I'm going to walk there from the beach. Is that okay?"

It's perfect," he says. "Now are you gonna kiss me?" He laughs as I kiss him. "Have a great day," he says as he walks away with Flounder following him. I wrap the sweater around me as I watch him walk away. I spend the day cleaning and dusting; there is so much dust. I don't see Crystal the whole day. Even when I go upstairs to take a relaxing bath, the door to her room stays closed. I take out my white jeans with a chiffon white tank top and pair it with a cream-colored sweater. I take out a gold necklace and put some mascara and a light pink lip gloss on. I grab my ballerina shoes and the cherry pie I bought, then lock up and make my way down the beach to Jensen's house.

I walk along the shore, slowly taking in the waves as my mind fills with Jensen and his kisses. I feel like a teenager going over to her boyfriend's house. The butterflies float all over my stomach, and my hands get tingly. The wind blows in my hair, and I finally make my way up his walkway. His house is huge; I never actually looked at it before. I walk to the back and see him sitting slouched back in a wooden chair. His black jeans, worn perfectly, and his black tight V-neck long-sleeved shirt molds his chest and is pulled up a bit, showing me his black belt. The open button at the V-neck gives me a glimpse of his chest. "There you are," he says as he gets up and makes his way to me. "I tried to text you," he says.

"Oh, I left my phone at home. I didn't think I needed it." I shrug. Ever since I moved here, I rarely have my phone on me. "Did you need something?" I ask him as he stands in front of me.

"Yeah," he says, raising his arm and scratching the back of his neck. His shirt lifts, so I catch a glimpse of his toned stomach. "You." He leans in to kiss my lips, leaving enough room for the pie.

"Really?" I grab his hands and intertwine our fingers, laughing as we make our way to the house. "Your backyard is almost like a resort. I was here before, but I was carrying Mila and didn't have time to look around." I say as I look at the huge pool with a rock wall, hiding a slide.

"Good," he says as he makes his way through a door that brings me to this huge great room. The high ceilings boast exposed wooden beams. A rock wall with a fireplace and a television right over it. Big leather couches sit in the middle of the room. "This is the great room."

I look around. "It really is a great room." I smile as he walks to the kitchen, which is right behind the great room, the whole room open. The kitchen cabinets are a dark wood, the counters a black granite. A big island in the middle has four stools around the front. The appliances are all stainless steel. He walks to the fridge that must be at least seven feet tall. "I thought we could have baked potatoes with the steaks."

I lean against the island. "That sounds delicious." I place the pie down on the counter. "What can I do to help?" I ask as he takes out four steaks and brings them over to the counter. "Are we having company?" I ask, a little sad that it won't be just the two of us.

"No." He smiles as he puts them on the counter. "I just got extra in case you're a big eater."

I shove his shoulder as he laughs out loud, turning to get the potatoes and a glass bowl. "You can prepare the potatoes, and I'll marinate the meat." He sets the potatoes on the counter with the aluminum foil. I walk behind the island and stand next to him as he prepares the steak, tearing off the foil to wrap the four potatoes tightly. I'm looking down as my shoulder touches his arm, but then I look over at him. He reaches his arm around me, his hand cupping my neck, and he brings me close to him, bending down to kiss me. The butterflies start in my stomach and spread throughout me. He tilts his head as he comes close to my face, and I open my mouth to kiss him. His warm tongue invades my mouth, and I groan into him. My heart beats fast as my stomach drops, and he kisses me softly and passionately. He pulls back, leaving me breathless, wanting more, aching for more. "I've been waiting to do that all day."

"Me too," I whisper as he comes close again and pecks my lips, leaving them tingling. He turns to get a baking sheet and then places the potatoes in the oven.

"Want to go sit outside? It should be ready in an hour." I nod, and he opens the fridge. "Do you want something to drink? A beer, wine?"

"I'll have wine if you have it." He grabs a beer, then walks over to the other side of the island and opens another fridge, pulling out a bottle of wine. He turns to grab a wine glass.

We walk past the couches again, and he goes out another door off the side.

"Holy shit," I say as I take in this side of the back-yard. Its wooden roof covers the whole area, and the floor is all pieces of different rocks. To one side, there is a table with big brown chairs, and to the other side is a seating area with a matching couch set. Potted plants are everywhere. The barbecue is situated behind a half brick wall but is still covered. Tea lights are all over the place and slowly lighting up the area as the sun starts to set. He walks over to the table where he opens the wine bottle and hands me a glass. "Is that a hammock?" I ask him as I look in the yard and see two trees holding up what looks like a hammock.

"It is." He nods as he opens his beer. "No one really uses it, though."

"I think I would lie in it every single day. I love hammocks," I say as he walks over to the couch and sits down. I walk to the edge of the rock floor and look to my left. "Is that a hot tub all by itself?"

"Yes." He nods his head. "It's right outside my room." My stomach fills again as I picture him in it naked. I take a sip of wine to stop myself from asking him if he goes in it naked.

I turn and walk to him as I sit beside him and tuck my legs under me. "So tell me something about Jensen I don't know."

He laughs. "I sleep naked when Mila isn't here." He winks at me as my pulse speeds up. "What about you?"

I take a sip of courage, oh, I mean wine. "I sleep naked every single night," I say as his jaw stays tight. I lean in. "Naked, naked." I giggle when he glares at me. "Don't play the game if you can't handle the heat."

"Oh, I can handle the heat," he says and then looks out at the horizon. "This is the first date I've been on since Julia left." He looks over as my mouth closes, and I swallow the feeling like something is stuck. "I just wanted you to know that I don't do this"—he points to him and me as he takes a pull of his beer—"ever."

"Why me?" I ask the obvious question.

"Because I know you won't play games with me. I know that if you let me in, it's genuine and real." He puts his hands on my leg. "And honestly, I can't get you out of my head."

I take a gulp of wine, or rather, I finish the whole glass, then lean over him and place it on the side table as his eyes grow darker. "I won't play games with you, and I know you won't play games with me either. I didn't come here expecting to find you." I wipe my eye before a tear comes out, blinking the tears away.

"I didn't expect to find myself, let alone someone who makes my heart flutter."

"I make your heart flutter?" His hand comes up to cup my cheek, and I lean into the touch.

"When you aren't an asshole, yes." I laugh as he smiles. "It doesn't hurt that you're easy on the eyes."

"Were you checking me out?" He smirks.

"I can't guarantee you anything." I swallow, looking down at my hands as they tap together. "I don't know when I'm going to be ready for the next step, but …"

He places his finger on my lips. "How about we just take this one day at a time?"

I smile and then kiss his finger. "I like that." I lean in. "But with kissing, right? Because I really like kissing you."

"Good." He grabs my face as I lean over him. "Because there is a fuck load of kissing that will be happening," he says right before he tilts his head and nips at my bottom lip. "In fact"—he kisses the side of my mouth—"I think we should practice right now." He kisses the other side as my stomach pulls tight. "Actually, after dinner I think we should practice on the couch." His tongue comes out to lick my bottom lip. His mouth devours mine, and my tongue dances with his. I climb into his lap, and we practice kissing till we are both breathless and itching with need. "I'm going to go check on the potatoes before I throw all the promises I made you out the window."

I think that is a great idea. I'm going to go visit the restroom." I follow him inside, and he points at the door across the room. I walk into the bathroom, close the door, and then collapse on the back of it, willing my heart to slow. Pushing off, I turn on the cold water. Wetting my hands, I pat my cheeks and look up. Little red dots are all around my mouth from his beard, and I smile at my reflection. My index fingers trace them; I'm loving them on me. My eyes that were dull a couple of months ago now sparkle, and the creases around them are back from smiling so much. "I'm happy," I whisper to myself in the mirror. Turning off the light, I go in search of the man who helped bring some of the light back.

Chapter Nineteen
Jensen

I breath in, and something tickles my nose as I shake my head side to side and open my eyes. Looking down, I see blond hair. My arm under me is asleep, my body stiff as the other arm hugs Hailey's waist. I pull back a bit and see her sleeping with one hand under her cheek and the other around my waist.

Last night, we ate outside, telling each other stories about our childhood. She told me stories about her and Crystal and her brother, Blake. My stories always involved Gabe and Brody. I brought her to the hammock after we finished eating, and we lay there with each other, her head on my chest, and looked up at the stars. Not a word was said; it was just the two of us lost in our own world. When it got too cold, we walked inside. The time got later and later, but neither of us wanted the night to end. We lay on the couch as I put a movie on, but the last thing we did was watch the movie. We kissed each other senseless. The kisses never stopped as we drifted off to sleep, only to wake in the middle of the night with the need to touch each other, and then we drifted off again.

"You suck at pretending to be asleep," I hear her say as I look down. She put her hands over her head and stretches as my hand brings her closer to me, and I roll on top of her.

"I wasn't pretending; I was listening to you snore," I tell her as I lean down and kiss her lips as she smiles. "I think you drooled on my shirt." My nose rubs against her jaw, and she opens her legs for me to settle between them, my cock bursting to get out.

Her hands roam up my chest as she rubs my shoulders and groans. "I do not snore."

"Oh baby, you snore." I kiss her chin. "Softly." I kiss her chin again softly, moving it along. "You also make this little noise," I tell her as her legs wrap around mine, "almost like a moaning." Her breath hitches as she swallows, and as I watch her neck move, I bend to kiss it, sucking in gently. "So you see." I keep kissing her neck, moving up to her lips. "That is why I didn't wake you."

"Really?" she says as I look at her. "I tho—" She stops midsentence because a gasp fills the room, and I look over to see Norma standing in the middle of the room. "Oh, my god." I hear Hailey whisper under me as she pushes me away from her, and I fly up off the couch, eyeing Norma.

"Norma." My voice comes out harsh as I get up and try to shield Hailey even though we are both fully dressed. "What are you doing here?" I ask her as I drag my hand through my hair.

"I thought I would come by and see if Mila wanted to take a walk on the beach. I didn't know you would be entertaining a guest." The venom dripping from her tongue makes my body goes tight, and I feel Hailey tense also.

"I should go," she whispers from behind me as her hands leave my waist and she looks for her shoes.

"Maybe you should," Norma says, and I snap as I see the shocked look on Hailey's face.

"She isn't leaving. You are." I look at Norma, who looks shocked. "And from now on, you call before coming over."

Her hands entwine as she holds them together. "Is this how you plan on raising my granddaughter, with a revolving door?"

"Yup, we are done here," I yell. "You don't get to tell me how to raise my daughter." I stand there, pulling Hailey to my side. "No one does. That's the joy of having her mother sign away all rights to her," I say as Norma's eyes go to slits.

"Julia could still change her mind." She stands there as I put my hand up.

"I don't give a shit if she changes her mind or not, Mila's mine. Not hers. She has two other children she chose to raise."

"I'm not going to discuss my daughter in front of a stranger," she says.

"We aren't discussing anything. From now on, you

call before you come into my home," I tell her, thinking I need to change the locks anyway.

She looks over at Hailey then back at me and then back at her again. "Don't get too comfortable. My daughter will be back, and she will take her rightful place as his wife."

"Ex," Hailey says from beside me, "his ex-wife." Norma doesn't say anything, so Hailey holds my hand, and she squeezes it and smiles. "From what I heard, she threw him away along with her beautiful girl." Norma nods, then turns and walks out of the house, slamming the door behind her. "I'm sorry, I had to say something." She looks at me as I try to get my anger under check.

"You're sorry?" I laugh sarcastically. "You're sorry? Fuck, I'm the one who needs to be sorry for bringing that woman into your life." She shakes her head. "She crossed so many lines by saying all those things. This conversation with her isn't over; I can tell you that."

"I'm not the other woman," she says quietly from beside me. My body goes solid, and ice fills my blood, and I have a hatred stronger than when Julia left. I walk to her, grabbing her face.

"You are not the other woman," I tell her as she nods her head and tears form in her eyes. "You will never be the other woman again. Ever." Her tears fall on my hands, and they soak into my skin. "I promise you will never cry because of that bullshit again." I kiss her cheeks where her tears just rolled off.

"Okay," she whispers, her voice cracking as the

perfect night got drowned out by the nastiness of this morning.

"I really want to forget this just happened, but I know we won't." I kiss her lips. "Last night was the best night I've had in a long, long time."

"Me too," she says as her hands go to my waist and she holds on to my belt. The doorbell fills the room as I put my head back and count to ten in my head. Brody walks into the room with Darla, but they stop in their tracks when they see us in the middle of the room.

"Well, fuck me," Brody says as Darla just looks stunned, "we brought doughnuts."

"What is wrong with everyone today?" I say under my breath as Hailey laughs. My hands drop from her face, and I stand next to her, not sure what to do, but she surprises me by linking our hands together.

"Holy shit," Darla says still stuck at her spot, "we are so sorry."

Brody looks at her as he puts the box down on the counter. "Why are we sorry? They aren't naked. So." He walks around and starts the coffee. Then the door opens again, and Gabe walks in, taking in the four of us.

"What the fuck? Is this a meeting?" he asks as he walks to the doughnut box, opening it up and taking one out. A knock on the back door has us all turning to find Crystal looking in. "Fuck," I hear Gabe say as he bites again and swallows. Hailey walks over to the door, opening it.

"Seriously, you can't go out without your phone.

I was texting you all night," she says as Gabe starts coughing with a fist in front of his mouth.

"You spent the night?" he asks as he continues to cough. "I need water," he says as he opens the fridge and takes out a beer. "Why are you here?" He points at Crystal.

"I was making sure she was okay. Why are you here?" She folds her arms over her chest.

"This is my cousin's house," he says, and we all look from one to the other like it's a tennis match.

"Well, my cousin went out for dinner, and it's breakfast, so …" she says, tossing her hair behind her shoulder.

"So you thought you would cock block her?" He smirks. "Nice."

"I wasn't cock blocking her; I was making sure she was okay. Why are you here? Did your date wake up and notice what an asshole you were?"

"I told you, she wasn't a fucking date." He smashes the can of beer in his hand.

"Whatever. I couldn't care less." She rolls her eyes at him, and I look at my cousin and see he is about to throw that can and smash my wall.

"Okay," I say as I clap my hands together. "Who wants breakfast?" I ask, looking around. "Darla?" I ask her as she looks like she is in another world.

"I'm sorry." She blinks her eyes. "She spent the night?" She points at Hailey. "And Gabe wants Crystal?"

"I don't want her," Gabe says at the same time Crystal yells out, "Oh, he doesn't want me," and they glare at each other.

"I actually slept on the couch," Hailey says, "and nothing happened." I wrap my hand around her shoulder, and I bring her to me and kiss her head.

"Honey," Darla says to Brody. "I think we need to go outside and walk back inside," she whispers as he bends down to kiss her.

"I would love, love to eat something," Crystal says as she walks into the kitchen and grabs a doughnut. "I can make the toast." She chews on a piece of doughnut. "Hailey makes the best pancakes of life."

"I can make pancakes," she says as she wraps her hand around my waist.

"I can make the bacon," Brody says.

"I can set the table," Darla says

"That means you can leave." Crystal looks at Gabe. "You might have another date waiting." She smirks at him.

"I'm not leaving." He crosses his arms over his chest. "Me and you are going to have words later," he says, and the way he speaks, I know I don't want to be part of that conversation.

"I don't have to speak to you before Monday," she says as she turns to face him, "so I guess we can talk then." He walks to her, and when she looks up at him, he bends over, picks her up, and throws her over his shoulder.

"Now." He carries her into the backyard as she howls, but only gets two feet away.

"You asshole. You're hurting me," she yells, and he stops and puts her down. You could see the horror in his eyes.

"Where are you hurt?" he asks as he checks her out, and she slaps his hands away.

"You hurt my stomach," she says as she tries to shoo him away.

"I didn't mean to." His voice going soft, he touches her stomach, and she lets him.

"Holy shit," Darla says again. "It's like aliens have invaded our city." They look inside, and Crystal walks past him, breaking the moment.

"Are we going to eat or not?" she asks as she opens the fridge and takes out a water bottle. No one says anything as we watch Gabe look at the sky and say something under his breath. We all go into the kitchen and take our places to try to cook breakfast. The saying too many cooks in the kitchen is in fact the right one. With every turn, we were bumping into someone. We finally finished and all ate outside.

After we clean up, we're all standing around the kitchen. Brody and Darla are the first to leave, kissing us all goodbye. Darla smirks at me the whole time. "You dirty dog, you," she whispers in my ear.

"Let's go," Gabe tells Crystal as he gets up.

"No, thanks," she tells him as she turns and walks out the back door, slamming it on the way.

"That fucking woman is going to be the death of me," he says as he turns to walk out the front door, slamming it. I look at Hailey, and she looks at me, and then we hear the door open again and watch as Gabe runs through the house to the back where he slams the door while yelling Crystal's name.

We both look at each other, shaking our heads. "Come on," I tell her as I grab her hand and walk back to the couch. "I want to kiss you again."

"Really?" she says. "Aren't you sick of me yet?" she asks as I look at her.

"Not even close," I tell her as I kiss her lips, and we fall onto the couch.

Two days later, I'm still replaying the weekend in my head. Her taste still on me as my cell phone rings, and I see it's Jessica.

"Hey," I say as I answer.

"Walker," she says, whispering. "Norma is here, and I think you need to come home." I get up from my desk as I walk to my truck.

"What's going on?" I ask her as I hear rustling in the background.

"She showed up and tried to come in with her key, but it obviously it didn't work," Jessica says as I start driving home. I had the locks changed the next day. "Anyway, she insisted she see Mila. I didn't think anything of it till she took her to her room and ..." She stops talking, and my blood turns cold. I think I see black, but all I know is that I couldn't get home fast enough.

"And what, Jessica?" I yell.

"She didn't know that the baby monitor was still on, so she just started asking her questions ..." Jessica stops talking. "About you and Hailey."

"Jessica, I'm there in two minutes. You do not let her leave. When I get there, I'm going to need you to take Mila for a walk, for ice cream, I don't care, but I want her out of the house,"

I tell her as I disconnect the phone. Turning in the driveway, I run into the house and see Jessica in the kitchen, her face white as she has just seen a ghost and she points toward Mila's room.

I walk into the room, stopping at the doorway as I see Norma and Mila sitting on the floor playing Barbies. "So if she comes…" Norma is talking as she looks up, but then she sees me in the doorway, and the blood rushes from her face.

"Hey," I say as Mila looks up and jumps, running for me.

"Poppa." I kiss her neck, putting her down.

"Say goodbye to Grandma Norma. Jessica is going to take you out for ice cream," I tell her as she cheers and runs to go find Jessica. Shouting goodbye over her shoulder to her grandmother.

Norma gets up from the floor and stands in the middle of the room. I wait for the sound of the front door closing before I speak.

"What are you doing here?" I ask her, giving her a chance to see if she will tell me the truth.

"I came to speak to my granddaughter. I missed her," she says.

"Soo, you didn't try to use your key to get in, a key I told you not to use again?" I ask her as fury takes over.

"You weren't really serious about that, were you?" She laughs.

"I was as serious," I start. "I was as serious as when I told you that you would not get to see her if you didn't abide by my rules."

"Those rules were four years ago. What is this?" she starts asking.

"I have to say I really wish I didn't have to do this." Norma starts to say something, but I put my hand up. "I warned you, the minute I thought you were playing games with Mila, it would end. Your visits would end. It started when you kept Julia's picture, with her twins, up on your fireplace mantle when she visited, and I told you to take it down. Then you come over here and ask her questions that are none of your business."

"What goes on with my granddaughter is my business."

"She isn't your granddaughter," I throw at her, and she gasps in shock that I would go there.

"It ends here. No more visits, no more nothing. You want to see her, call me and I'll set it up that you are at the same restaurant as us. Other than that, until Mila is old enough to decide whether she wants to see you, that is how it's going to work."

"All this for her. You've known that woman for five minutes."

"You don't get to question me, but just to put your mind at ease I'll tell you. Your daughter left me, shattering me, and day in and day out that shattered man healed, but then the hatred set in. I hate her, but not because she was a coward and just left me. No, I hate her for not loving her daughter enough to fight me for her. Every day, my daughter smiles at me, and I couldn't imagine leaving her and just saying see you later. Especially for someone else." I sigh and then smile. "She's the first girl since Julia who makes me want more. She is the first one who I ever thought about dating; fuck, she is the first one I want to take that chance with. She is the first one who looked past the man who was left behind."

"She is going to change her mind," Norma says, "Julia is going to see reason."

"I don't fucking care if she changes her mind and comes crawling back on her hands and knees begging for forgiveness. I don't want her. It's been four years. It's not going to happen. I will not let her near my daughter. Not now, not ever."

"You can't stop her."

"Get out." I shake my head. "Get out. I'm done here. This is over." I turn to walk into the living room, and Norma follows me out.

"You'll change your mind," she says as she walks toward the door.

"Not a chance in hell because, you see, I have one job, and that job is to protect my daughter, even if it's from you."

She nods at me as she walks out the door, and I'm left to wonder if she finally gets it.

Chapter Twenty
Hailey

"I should go," I say three weeks after our first kiss. "If Mila gets up and I'm still here, there may be questions." I smile at him as I get on my tippy toes to kiss his lips.

"But I don't want you to go," he whines as he wraps his arms around my waist and kisses my lips and then my neck.

We have been going very slow. After his talk with Norma, he sat down with Mila and told her that we were friends and that I would be around more. Mila, of course, did what every four-year-old did; she shrugged her shoulders and asked if she could have cake before dinner. I've been over a couple of times. We don't kiss in front of her, but when she goes to sleep, all bets are off. When I don't have dinner with them, I walk over after, just so I can hug him. I don't even need to kiss him. I lie … I need him to kiss me.

I smile at the thought of him, and sometimes I sit at my desk and just think about him. It's come so easy, and naturally, it feels like it was always like this. That the pain we've both felt was in another lifetime.

"The sun is coming up," I tell him as I kiss him one last time and walk out the back door. He stands in his jogging pants and t-shirt watching me leave. I'm familiar with his whole body. We haven't been under the clothes yet, but I know his ridges, and I know his firmness—I actually know his firmness really well since he's constantly firm around me. I breathe in the warm air; it's getting warmer now. I walk down the wet sand as I make my way around the bend, the seagulls out in full force today. The wind blows my hair in all sorts of directions. I look at the mist of the water as it splashes on my face. Walking up to my back door, I push it open and head inside, taking off my Uggs before stepping into my bedroom.

I look at the clock and see it's almost seven, then hear some noise coming from the kitchen. Cupboards being banged. I walk into the kitchen and gasp when I see Gabe in the kitchen, obviously searching for a coffee cup.

"What are you doing here?" I walk to the side where we keep the coffee mugs.

"Your cousin wasn't answering her phone last night, so ..." He starts talking when Crystal comes in.

"So he decided coming here at one a.m. and throwing rocks at my window was a good idea." She opens the fridge, getting out the milk and her lunch bag.

"I wouldn't have to do that if you had just answered your phone." He pours himself coffee, and as I take in his jeans and t-shirt, the tattoos on his arm seem bigger.

"There was no need to answer my phone." She shrugs, taking out some cereal and pouring it into a bowl.

"Because you hate being wrong." He points at her, and her eyes narrow. The box of cereal smashes on the counter.

"I'm leaving," she says, grabbing her purse, keys, and lunchbox. Turning to me, she says, "Blake should be here late today. He called last night."

I nod at her as happiness fills me. I haven't seen my brother in over two months and so much has changed. "Oh, you answered his phone call!" Gabe says when he grabs his jacket and heads to the front door where Crystal stands.

"Well, he isn't an asshole," she counters when she opens the front door. "How are you getting to work?" she asks him when he laughs.

"You are going to drive me. I took a cab last night."

"I'm not showing up with you in my car." She turns on him. "People will see."

"And that's a problem because?" He puts his hands on his hips. "What's the matter, babe? Scared they might think you have a thing for me?"

She shakes her head, laughing. "Trust me, the last thing I have is a thing for you."

"I'll remember that the next time you are beg—" She runs to him, covering his mouth with her hand.

"Get in, I'm dropping you off at the corner. I'll slow down so you can tuck and roll." He smacks her ass as she turns, earning a glare from her. "I won't even slow down now."

Gabe throws his head back laughing as he gets in the car and leans over to kiss her. What has me raising my eyebrows is that she lets him. Crystal has always said she is never getting married, never settling down. She adamantly insists she is happy being alone. She crossed kids off her list when she turned nineteen, vowing to be the best aunt she could possibly be. I watch her drive off as Gabe picks up her hand and kisses it, smiling at her.

"That poor, poor man. He has a better chance landing on the moon than changing her mind." Shaking my head, I walk back inside, putting the cups in the sink and the cereal box away. I grab my laptop and head upstairs to my office to answer emails when I hear a knock on the front door. Walking to it, I open it and see my brother's smiling face.

I leap into his arms, and he catches me in his big strong arms. I bury my face in his neck as tears come to my lids. Not sad tears, just happy, happy that he's here. "You're here," I say when he lets me go. I step back, giving him room to come in, carrying his bag in with him.

"Look at you." He points at me. "You look amazing. The fresh beach air suits you."

"I think so." I smile when he comes in and looks around. "This is my home." Looking around, I see that it really is mine.

"Looks amazing." He walks to the fireplace and

picks up a picture of Crystal and me taken last weekend when we went to the farmers market. "You guys look like this is where you're meant to be." He puts the frame down and walks to the kitchen. "I'm starving." Grabbing some leftovers from last night, he pops them in the microwave, then leans back on the counter. "So what else is new?"

The question is a loaded one, and he doesn't even know. I haven't told anyone about Jensen, only because I'm not sure what to say. "Nothing really." I shrug. The microwave beeping saves me this time. I know by the time he leaves, he will know all about Jensen. "Did you come here right after your shift?"

He nods his head as he digs into the pasta. "I'm bone dead tired. If you don't mind, I'm going to take a shower and crash for a couple of hours."

"Mi casa es su casa." *My house is your house.* I joke with him. "There is a twin bed upstairs, but you won't fit in it, so you can have my bed."

"You sure?" he asks as he puts the container in the sink, and I nod. He kisses my cheek. "You look fantastic." He looks into my eyes when I smile.

"Go, we will catch up later," I tell him, pointing at the hallway where my room and the shower are. I walk back upstairs to my office when I hear the shower running. Opening my browser, I start working on the website for Heidi and Delores. I have all the things lined up when I hear a soft knock on the door. Getting up, I walk downstairs, but Blake beat me to the door. He swings the door open as he stands there shirtless and in his shorts. My mouth opens as I see Jensen standing there glaring. "Who the fuck are you?" he asks as Blake now stands up straight, his muscles going tight.

"Who the fuck am I? Who the fuck are you?" he hisses. I run down the stairs and step in front of Blake and smile to a white-faced Jensen, taking in his fists beside him.

"This is Blake," I tell him, trying to get him to look at me and not Blake. "My brother," I say, the words finally clicking as he looks at Blake and then down at me.

"Oh," he says as I turn to look at Blake. "This is Jensen Walker."

Blake doesn't say anything and just nods, and Jensen puts his hand out. "My friends call me Walker; your sister and my grandmother are the only ones who call me Jensen." Blake reaches out to shake his hand. They both stand there, eyeing each other.

"Okay," I say when I push my brother so his hand releases from Jensen. "You were going to nap, so go."

He looks at me and then at Jensen. "I'll see you around."

Jensen just puts his chin up, accepting the invitation. Blake walks back toward my room as I watch him and then turn back to look at Jensen. "So what brings you by?" I say, leaning against the door. The sight of him in his dusty work clothes, thick sweater, and construction boots have me almost fanning myself.

"Well, I was in the neighborhood, and I thought I would swing by and get—"

I smile, walking to him. "You thought you would get what, exactly?" I wrap my arms around his shoulder as his hand grasps my waist, bringing me to him.

He leans in, kissing me. "Some of this." He kisses the side of my lips, then down to my neck. I move my head to the side to give him full access right before he comes up and takes my lips.

"Well," I say when we pull apart. "You can pass by anytime for that," I tell him as I bury my face in his shoulder.

"I guess you aren't going to come down tonight?" he asks when I look behind me.

"Not sure, but I might be able to sneak over just to get some." I wiggle my eyebrows at him as he smiles, kissing me once again before turning to walk back to his truck.

I lean on the doorjamb, checking him out. "Nice ass, Walker," I shout, and he turns and looks over his shoulder.

"I could say the same," he says. Climbing in his truck, he drives away. I close the door.

"So he's the reason you look like you do?" Blake asks, standing in the doorway to my bedroom. I walk over to the kitchen and grab a bottle of water from the fridge. My throat suddenly dry like sand.

"I don't know what you mean," I tell him, avoiding his eyes.

"Your glow, your eyes, shine." He walks into the kitchen and takes a seat at the table. "I was expecting to come here and find the shell of a woman who had her heart broken. The defeated look you had when you packed up your car and took off." He puts his hands on the table. "I expected to see you withdrawn. I expected to see you locked away."

"Well," I start but stop when he lifts his hand.

"I'm not saying it's a bad thing." He shakes his head. "Trust me, it's fucking great. I'm just surprised is all."

I nod, taking another sip of water, and walk to the kitchen table. Pulling out the chair and sitting down in front of him, I know I have to give him the truth. "I will be honest … when I got here, I was broken, empty, shallow. I felt like I wouldn't be able to go on the next day. It was like I was the one who was dead. I was the one buried in a box with everything crashing down on me, crushing me. Every single time I took a breath, my chest hurt; my heart beat, but nothing else came out of it. It was beating to beat. But then I came into this broken-down house, and let me tell you, it was broken down. I thought Crystal was going to hightail it back home, but I went to the beach and I sat down on the cold sand, the waves crashing into the shore, and I felt as lost as the waves did. But then I felt something else even though at the time I didn't know what. Now that I look back, I think I just felt at peace. So even if the house was in shambles, I knew this was where I wanted to be. It was where I had to be. So I moved in and the house was a disaster, but in a weekend, it was perfect." I swallow. "And every day, I used to sleep maybe two, three hours tops, but I would wrap myself in a blanket and go outside, and I would watch the waves crash into the shore. I would think of all the little things Eric did to try to understand why." I look down at my hands, thinking of how far I've come. "I would wonder what I could have done differently to be that person he needed. Or I would try to see if I missed any signs he had another woman. I mean seriously"—I laugh but the tears get me also—"how could I not know he was with another woman? How could I not see the lies that came out of his mouth? How could I not be that one person who made him complete?" I swallow as Blake squeezes my hands.

"You were not the problem," he tries, but I stop him.

I nod my head. "Oh, I know that now, but I didn't back then. I went through every memory and dissected it to see if I missed something. A clue, a word, something to see if it was in front of my face this whole time, but"—I shake my head as my thumb wipes away a tear in the corner—"but it wasn't there. No matter what I did, I couldn't see it then, and I couldn't see it now. I loved him. I really did, with all my heart, but then I hated him." I swallowed past the lump in my throat. "I hate him. I hate him more than I loved him. And I hate that I hate him; I hate that he did this to me. That he took what I thought was the love of my life and made me hate it. I hate that he took the love I gave him and made it into a lie."

"It wasn't all like that. He did love you." Blake reaches out, and I put one hand on top of his.

"No, he didn't because if he did, he would never

have done what he did." I shake my head. "He would never promise to love me till we grow old together when he already made those promises to someone else. When he already promised her more. Fuck, he had children with this woman." I throw my hands up. "You see, he didn't love me. He was just selfish. He didn't love me; he loved himself."

"Hailey ..." he says.

"No," I slam my hand on the table. "There are no words you can say that will make what he did okay. Nothing you can do or say will change my mind on that. There are no pictures you paint that will make it okay, but"—I inhale—"with all these memories and thoughts, I came to a conclusion. I deserve the fucking world. I deserve to have a man who will not only love me and only me but also won't have to look elsewhere to be complete. That is what I deserve. I deserve to be put on top of the pedestal and kept there."

"You think that guy can do it?" Blake points at the door.

I inhale and answer the loaded question as honestly as I can. "All I know is that I would never have to doubt Jensen. I know he calls me just because. I know when he has a shitty day, he talks to me about it instead of saying, 'I don't want to talk about it.' I know he would ever take off for work and not call at least once a day, and most of all, I know he would never lie to me. I haven't known him that long, but I know in here"—I point at my chest—"that my heart trusts him. That what he says is what he means. And that means everything," I tell him, and he nods at me.

"There are some things I need to tell you." He starts off, looking at me and then down at our hands. "Things that happened after you left that you should know."

I pull my hands away from him as I eye him, and he gets up and goes to my room as I watch him disappear and then come back out with a white envelope. "Now, I want you to hear me out before you say anything." I look at him as he sets the envelope down in front of him, my eyes never leaving the bleak white envelope.

"Eric left you a letter," he says, and I gasp, my heart racing like a million horses running in a field. My hands fly to my lap, shielding itself from touching that white envelope. "A month after you left, Samantha showed up looking for you."

"What?" I whisper as my heart never does get back to a normal heartbeat.

"She went by your old house because that is the address Elliot gave her." He looks at me to see if he should continue or not. "The new owners gave her my name. She showed up at the firehouse."

"Why the fuck would she show up at my house?" I ask him, wondering what she was thinking.

"She isn't the evil one you think she is," he says as she looks down and something glitches in his eyes. "She had no idea anything was happening. Or that he was leading a double life."

"I'm finally fucking happy, so why can't he let me be fucking happy?" I say, pushing to get up from the table. "I don't fucking want that letter. I don't want to read it; I don't want it in my house," I say to the universe more than to Blake. "Better yet, I don't fucking care." I storm out the front door, slamming the door behind me. Angry I left my own house. Angry I let it get to me, but more so angry he has now tainted my table with his bullshit. I turn to walk to the back, down to the water, down to where I can find myself.

Chapter Twenty-One
Jensen

"Where are you?" Crystal asks me. I'm pulling up to the office when I answer my phone.

"Just got to the office," I answer, suddenly confused as to why she is calling me. "What's the matter?" My body goes tight, and my blood goes cold.

"I have no idea, but Blake just called me and asked me to give you a call. I don't have the details," she says as I start my car and make my way over to Hailey's. "But she's on the beach." I toss my phone on the seat as I turn on her street and park in the driveway. Her brother's sitting on the front porch swing.

"What happened?" I ask him as I stand in front of the house.

"She's on the beach," is all he says or all I hear because I'm running to the beach, running to her.

I see her sitting in the middle of the beach, all alone, the wind blowing her hair as the water looks like its crashing on her. I walk down the steps to her. Instead of sitting beside her, I sit behind her. Resting my legs on the outside of hers, I lean my body over her, almost protecting her from the wind that howls around us. My hands go to my knees. I expect her to have her shield up and be stiff, but instead, she leans into me. "Hey there," I say into her neck as I lean down and kiss her. Her sniffling indicates she's has been crying.

"Why?" she whispers as she looks at the water, never turning to me. "Why can't he let me be happy?"

My hands form fists as I think about how it might not go over well to beat the shit out of her brother. "Hailey."

"No," she shouts. "Trust me, this are not sad tears, these are angry tears. I finally fucking feeling like myself again." She wipes her eyes and pushes her hair aside. "No, that is wrong. I feel better than I ever felt, and he somehow comes up with a way to kick me down," she says as she wipes away another tear. "He was married, fucking married to someone else." I wrap my hands around her, bringing her closer to me; her heart pounding so fast under my hand I think it's going to come out of her chest.

"Hailey, breathe," I tell her. "Just breathe." I kiss her neck as she slowly starts to settle.

"He left a fucking letter," she says finally after her breathing evens out, and her heart rate returns to normal. "A white envelope and get this," she says. "His wife, his real wife, not the other wife he kept on the side, the real true wife brought it to me."

I let her vent, hating Eric more than is humanly possible. More than even Julia, and I hated her right down to the pit of my stomach. "I didn't read it."

"Do you want to read it?" I ask her as she turns in my arms to look at me. "No," she says. "Not one piece of me needs those words in my life."

"Then don't." I kiss her lips, and then her tear stained cheeks. "You get to do this on your own time, when you want to. Not when he wants."

"Yes." She leans into my shoulder, laying her head against it. "I'm going to do it on my time."

I nod my head. "When you want to." I smile at her as she closes her eyes, and I hold her, thinking about that white envelope and wondering if things will still be the same between us when she opens it. I sit out there holding her while she processes whatever it is she needs to process.

"Do you want to get pizza tonight?" she asks me. "We could grab Mila and eat it there." She looks at me.

"Yeah, you want to bring Blake?" I ask, knowing he won't be visiting for long. No matter what she is going through, she still needs to spend time with him.

"Yeah," she answers as she gets on her knees, facing me. "I'm happy." Her declaration makes me smile.

"I'm happy too." I grab her face and kiss her. She lets go to stand up and holds her hand out for me to take as she tries to pull me up. I laugh at her while she grunts. I finally stand up, linking our fingers together, and we walk back to her house. "I will see you soon." I kiss her nose. "Call you when I get Mila."

"I'll meet you there," she tells me as she turns and

walks up the stairs to the house.

I pick up the phone and see I have about fifteen missed calls from Crystal, so I press her number. "What the fuck is wrong with you two? Why can't you carry phones?"

"Because they don't want you to disturb them," I hear Gabe in the background while Crystal hisses at him.

"Mrs. Henderson is waiting for you to treat her hang nail. I'm assuming you can do that without a nurse," she hisses. "What happened to Hailey?" she asks me.

"I think it's best for her to tell you." I'm not going to break the trust I have with her. "I'm going to get Mila and then we are meeting for dinner at D'Amore."

"Oh, I want pizza. I'm coming too. What time?" she asks.

"I have no idea. Probably around six."

"Perfect. I'm off by then, so save me a place."

"Me too," Gabe yells from the background.

"You aren't invited."

"My cousin is going, so I can go the restaurant if I want, Crys. It's a public place."

"Whatever, but you aren't sitting with us. Maybe you can meet another date?"

"Oh my god, I dated her in fucking high school," he counters.

"Okay, are you guys done?" I ask the bickering duo.

"I'm not talking to him. I'll be there. See you at six," she finally says then disconnects. I shake my head, thinking of the dysfunction that must be going on at that clinic.

I pull up to the house, and when I walk in, I hear Mila giggle. "I'm home," I yell, so she turns and runs to me.

"Poppa." She kisses my cheek. "We make cookies."

"Did you?" I ask her, smiling at Jessica.

"We did, and I ate some cookie dough," she whispers. "It's a secret, so don't say anything." I laugh, setting her down to run back and finish the cookie she was eating before I walked in.

"We are going to grab some pizza tonight," I tell her as I grab the mail on the table. "Would you like that?"

"Hmm." She moans out between her bites of cookie.

Jessica leaves right before six, at the same time as Mila and I make our way to D'Amore. I texted Hailey, telling her I would see her at six. She responded with a kiss emoji.

As we finally walk into D'Amore, my eyes are scanning everyone when I see Hailey wave her hand at me. "Look, Hailey is here," Mila says when we walk toward her.

"Hey there, Princess Mila." She smiles at her, and I nod to her brother, Blake, who is sitting in front of her. "Mila, this is my brother, Blake. Blake, this is the coolest four-year-old, Princess Mila."

Blake smiles at Mila. "Nice to meet you, your highness." He bows his head as Mila laughs and asks for crayons.

"I'm not driving you home. I hope you know." I hear

Crystal's voice when she walks in. Looking around, she spots us.

"You have to drive me home," Gabe says while he follows her.

"Hey there," Crystal says, sitting down next to Mila and kissing her cheek. "Hello, Princess. Blake."

"What happened to you?" I ask Gabe when he pulls out the chair next to me and sits.

"Someone sliced my brand-new tires again," he says while he raises his hand to flag down the waitress. "Can I have two beers please?" he asks, then looks around the table. "Anyone else want anything?" Shrugging, he says, "That's it."

"You ordered two beers?" I ask him, laughing.

He puts his hands up. "I have two hands, and after the day I've had, I should have doubled that order."

Crystal picks up a menu and mumbles, "Maybe if you weren't such an a-hole, people wouldn't slice your tires." Gabe doesn't say anything; he just glares at her. I look at them and then turn my head to listen to Blake and Mila's conversation. She's asking him about fifty different questions about being a firefighter.

"Do you run into the fire and save people?" she asks, wide-eyed.

"Yup. Sometimes we have no choice," he tells her. "Once I had to climb a tree to save a kitten."

Mila gasps. "Did you find the mommy?"

Blake nods. "Yup and his brothers and sisters."

"I want a brother," Mila says. I look over at Hailey to see how she is doing and find her eyes already looking at me. I smile at her and nod my head to the side.

"I'm going to the bathroom," I say, pushing my chair back.

"I need to go also," Hailey says, getting up.

"Well, isn't that convenient," Gabe says as he downs one beer.

I shove at his shoulder as I walk to the back where the bathrooms are. I look behind us and in front of us, then grab her hand and sneak us into the maintenance closet next to the bathroom. Her giggles fill the room while she squeezes into me.

"Hello." I pull her to me, kissing her lips. Her body molds to me.

"Hello." She kisses me lightly, then snakes her hands around me to pull me closer to her, my mouth taking hers.

"It kills me to walk into a room and not be able to kiss you hello," I tell her, kissing her cheek and then trailing kisses down her neck as she laughs at me.

"We'd better get back out there," she whispers.

"Are you okay?" I ask her, looking into her eyes for the answer.

"I'm good." She smiles, and I see that she actually is fine. I grab her hand, then open the door, looking out to make sure no one is there when we walk out.

"Oh, good," Gabe says as we both sit down. "We ordered for you guys since you were in the 'bathroom'." He makes air quotes with his fingers, causing Blake to laugh. I smile at him and nod my head.

"Did you see the house that just went on the market?" Gabe looks at me. My head nods, remembering the For Sale sign on Norma's lawn. "Guess she got the point, right?"

The meal runs smoothly till the bill comes and everyone fights for it, well, everyone but Gabe. He sits there glaring at Crystal, who returns the glare with a big smile.

"Too late," Gabe says. "I already paid the bill." He gets up, looking at Crystal. "Let's go."

This doesn't bode well for her as she folds her hands over her chest. "I'm not driving you home."

Gabe shakes his head. "Let's go." Then he hisses out, "Please."

"Fine." She throws her napkin on the table. "This is the last time." She grabs her purse, saying bye to us as they walk out.

"This was fun," Blake says as his phone rings. When he looks down and sees the number, he excuses himself. "Hello." We hear him answer and then he walks out.

"Let's go, Mila," I tell her while she puts her crayons away, then jumps off her chair, coming over to my side to hold my hand.

We walk out looking around for Blake who raises his hand still talking on the phone. "Do you want me to wait with you?" I ask her. She shakes her head, seeing Mila yawn.

"No, go ahead," she tells me. I lean in and kiss her cheek, waving goodbye to Blake as I pick Mila up and walk to my truck.

Bedtime is fast since Mila is so tired. I'm in my room pulling my shirt off when I hear a faint knock on the back door. Walking to the door, I see it's Hailey. "Hey there." She comes in.

"Hi, yourself." I close the door, turning to look at her. "You snuck out?"

She eyes me up and down. I'm not one to boast, but I work hard to make sure the dad bod is never a reality. She has never seen me without my shirt. "Blake crashed as soon as we walked in." She walks closer to me, putting her hands on my stomach, making my body tremble from her cold hands. "I forgot to get a kiss good night," she whispers, the heat in her eyes. I lick my lips as her face inches closer to me. "Kiss me," she asks or maybe she demands—I don't know because my hands fly to her hair. I grab it in my fist and tilt her head back, claiming her mouth with mine. As we groan into each other's mouth, standing at the back door, I know that sooner rather than later I'm going to take her to bed.

When the alarm sounds softly, I groan and reach out for it. But my hand is pressed into my bed. I roll over, taking Hailey with me, her groan of frustration filling the room. My chest tickles from her hair. After attacking each other at the door, she refused to let me put on a shirt, so we made out on my bed most of the night. Until we fell asleep. "It's five thirty," I tell her, kissing her neck, and she mumbles something. It takes me ten more minutes to get her up, and when I kiss her goodbye, the sun is up, and it hurts to watch her walk away.

I pick up my phone, texting my mother.

Can you watch Mila this weekend?

I put my phone down and pour a cup of coffee. My phone rings. I grab it when I realize it's my mother.

"Hello, Mother," I say. Looking at the time, I see it's almost six. "You're up early."

"I could say the same to you. Busy day ahead?" she asks.

"Yeah, somewhat. I have a couple of jobs to check out. Nothing more than usual." I take a gulp of coffee.

"So how about I take Mila on Friday and bring her back Monday? It would give you a good break. You could grab the boys and go fishing."

Except the boys are the furthest thing from my mind. The only thing I'll be doing is learning every single partof Hailey. "Sounds great," I tell her, and we make plans for her to pick Mila up tomorrow. I make Mila breakfast as soon as she wakes, and my day goes by at a snail's pace. I get a text that night from Hailey asking about my day as soon as I put Mila down.

I don't bother texting her. "My day was long as fuck. How was yours?" I say when she answers.

"It was good, long also. I'm just climbing into bed. I have a killer headache."

"Do you, why?" I ask, going to my own room.

"No clue, maybe the computer." I hear rustling, knowing she is getting under the covers.

"So do you have plans for dinner tomorrow?" I ask her as I hear her laugh.

"Crystal and I are bringing Blake to check out the

local band at the pub."

"Oh, you'll like that," I tell her.

"Do you want to meet me there?" she asks.

I smile. "I would love to meet you there."

We talk for about an hour. I hear her voice getting lower and lower and then ever so soft, so I tell her sweet dreams. She whispers them back to me, and I stay on the line after she hangs up. She is on my mind the whole night, and I dream of her and her laugh. The next day, I rush through what has to get done. I'm just getting home when she texts me to meet her at seven.

I shower and change the sheets, hoping she'll come home with me tonight. I pull out my black jeans and brown long-sleeve shirt. Pulling the sleeves up, I grab my watch and run my fingers through my hair. I pull up to the pub five minutes after seven.

I walk in, not sure where she will be sitting, but my eyes don't move far because she is standing near the bar. My heart stops in my chest as she looks over her shoulder. "Holy fuck," I say to myself as I take her in. She is wearing the tightest pair of blue jeans ever invented. Her white shirt hangs off both shoulders, and her sleeves go all the way to her wrists. Her hair is in curls and pulled over one bare shoulder. I look down to see she is wearing tan strappy fucking heels. When she smiles at me, I see a gold choker on her thin neck. My cock spring into action as my jeans tighten so hard I thank god the lights are dim and hopefully no one can see me saluting.

As I make my way to her, she turns to talk to the

bartender, ordering something. "Hey," I say, my hand coming out to hold her hip, and she leans over to kiss my cheek.

"I'm all by myself," she tells me. "Blake left early, something about having a situation that required his help." The bartender returns with a glass of wine for her and a bottle of beer. "I ordered you a beer."

"You look beautiful," I tell her, my tongue dry from looking at her. She looks down, tucking a piece of hair behind her ear.

"Thank you," she whispers in my ear, leaning over to make sure I hear. "You look hot yourself." She smiles, taking a sip of wine. I look into her eyes and see a twinkle, and I'm wondering if she's thinking the same thing I'm thinking.

"Hey, you two," Crystal says, breaking our trance. I take a pull of my drink, turning to look at her cousin, and I almost spit out my beer. Holy fuck, Gabe is going to lose his shit. She's standing in front me wearing tight black jeans, and I mean tight,

but that's not the problem. It's the sheer black halter she's wearing without a bra. She throws her blond hair over her shoulder, putting her hand out to catch the bartender's eyes, and does she ever. "We need three shots of tequila," she says as she smiles at Pat, grabbing her credit card.

"That's okay. Pat, put everything on my tab," I say from beside her, and she smiles at me.

"Aren't you the sweetest." She looks at Hailey. "That shirt is the bomb." They trade stories of the day, my hand never leaving Hailey's hip. I look at the door, seeing Brody and Darla come in.

Darla spots us, waving her hand. "Holy fuck," she spits out when she gets closer and takes in Hailey and then Crystal. "Oh my god, I'm so happy I came tonight." She looks at Crystal. "That outfit is to die for. I need to borrow that top."

"Over my dead body," Brody says from beside her. "Not even just for me. Besides, I don't think it'll last the night," he says, looking away as two beers appear on the counter with the shots of tequila.

"Shots," Darla yells out, throwing her hand up, while Brody and I both throw our heads back and groan. The girls toss back the shots and order another round.

"One more and that's it," Hailey says from beside me.

"What?" Crystal and Darla both look at her, but Darla speaks. "You are no fun." As they take another shot of tequila. "Country Girl" begins to play, causing Darla to yell, "We need to dance."

Hailey finishes off her wine, then leans in and kisses me on the lips in front of everyone. "Be back."

I lean on the bar as I watch the three of them in the middle of the pub. Every man watches and some women join them while others just glare at them. "How much are we betting that Gabe is going to lose his shit," Brody says, grabbing his beer and draining it.

"I'm almost afraid to be here if he shows up." I groan when "Save a Horse" comes on.

"Oh, she's here." Brody points at Crystal. "So he's going to show up. Plus, I may have texted him and told him we are here." He laughs as Darla yells she's riding a cowboy tonight.

They stay on the dance floor till they are out of breath, then come back to the bar to order more shots. "Okay, fine," Hailey says. "One more." She then looks at me and winks.

"You having fun?" I ask her when she leans into me.

"I am." She smiles, picking up her shot, and eyes me while she licks her hand and puts salt on it. My cock springs to action, my eyes watching her every single move. She licks the salt, downs the shot, winces, and sucks on the lime. "That is gross."

I look at Darla and Crystal, who take another shot and chase it with a glass of water. The band takes the stage, causing the music to get louder. Hailey picks up the glass of white wine I ordered for her while she danced.

I'm about to lean in and say something to her when I hear, "What the fuck are you wearing?" hissed next to me, and Brody just laughs. Crystal turns around, putting a hand on her hip.

"An outfit." She glares at him.

"Is that right?" He puts his hands in his back pocket, his dress shirt buttons almost snapping off.

"I think I need another shot," she says when she takes in his look.

Darla sees the look Gabe is giving and claps her hands. "I'm so happy I didn't miss tonight," she says as they take another shot.

"I'm going to go to the bathroom," Hailey says, grabbing Crystal, and Darla follows them. Brody pushes a bottle of beer in Gabe's hand while his eyes never leave Crystal's back.

I'm about to take a sip of my beer when I see Kimberley. "Incoming," Brody says, when she spots me and raises her hand.

"Hey," she says breathlessly. "I didn't know I would see you here tonight." Coming to my side, she leans against the bar. "You look good."

"Um." I look at my hand and then back up, seeing her smile as she tucks her hair behind her ear.

"Is someone sitting here?" She points at the bar stool no one is actually sitting on.

"Actually, there is." I nod at her, but don't say anything else because Hailey's walking back from the bathroom. She stands next to me, my hand going out and automatically gripping her.

"Oh," Kimberley says, her eyes blinking a million times. "I didn't know you two ..."

"Hi." Hailey smiles at her. "We met, right?" She tilts her head, and I know my girl is not playing right now.

"Yeah, when you moved into town. I work for Walker," Kimberley tells her.

"That's right. You work for Jensen and Brody." She grabs her glass of wine.

"I see some friends," Kimberley says, walking away. Darla snickers. The band tells us they're going to slow things down and the guitar riff starts.

"Come on, cowboy," Darla says, "you owe me a dance." He follows her to the crowded dance floor.

"You want to dance?" I ask Hailey. She grabs my

hand and pulls me to the dance floor. I take her in my arms, and even with her heels on, I'm still just a bit taller. Her hand goes around my neck, and one of my hands wrapping around her waist. I look over at Gabe, who is following Crystal outside. He makes sure I see him, waving at us.

"There goes my ride." Hailey smiles at me.

"Come home with me." Four words. Four words that hang in the air. Four words that mean so much while she looks down and then up.

"Okay." She leans in and whispers in my ear, "Only if I get to sleep over."

Chapter Twenty-Two
Hailey

We say goodbye to Darla and Brody, walking out. Lost in our own thoughts, we remain quiet on the way to his house. Butterflies fill my stomach, my heart feels like it's going to explode in my chest, my body aware of every time his hand touches me as he drives. From the way his thumb moves on my thigh to the way he picks up my hand and brings it to his lips.

Parking the car, he looks over at me, and I smile. My hand reaches for the handle to open the door, and I step out of the truck. Jensen walks around the back of the truck to my side. I turn to look at him, but he backs me up against the truck. The cool metal on my back causes me to arch into him a bit. His hands bury in my hair, and he pulls my face to his, his lips on mine, his tongue dancing with mine. The kiss leaves me wanting so much more, aching for him, aching for his touch. We walk with his arm around my neck and my arms wrapped around his waist, and when we reach the front door, he reaches into his pocket to get the keys out. Opening the door, only a dim light glows as we walk across his house to his bedroom. A bedroom I've been in about a hundred times now, but knowing what is to come makes my palms start to sweat.

He stops us when we get to the doorway of his room and turns me toward him. He leans in and kisses my bare shoulder, the prickle of his beard making me shiver. "There is no pressure; there is no rush," he tells me, trailing kisses from my shoulder to my neck. "It's just me and you." He kisses up my neck. My palms lie flat against his chest, and I feel his heart beating almost as fast as mine. "I want you," he whispers as his tongue trails up and down my neck, "but at any time." He sucks a bit, and I arch my back into his touch. He stops kissing me and looks at me, his thumb tracing my bottom lip. "We go at your pace," he says, looking into my eyes. "I don—" My hand stops him from talking.

"Nothing in this world can stop this from happening. There is nothing in this world I want more than to be with you"—I inhale—"completely with you." I move closer to him, our chests connected, the heat from both of us seeping into each other. I wrap my hands around his neck, giving myself a little bit more courage, our heart beat against each other, his hands on my hips. "So are you going to kiss me or not?" I smile as the words come out, but then his lips crash into mine. His hands grab my ass, pulling me to him. Turning me, he backs me into his room until the back of my legs hit the bed, our mouths never leaving each other. My hands roam down the front of his chest to the hem of his shirt. I pull his shirt up, my fingertips working their way up his six-pack. He trails kisses from my face to my neck, then back up to my ear. The sting from his beard makes my one of my shoulders rise up, my hands now pushing his shirt up, but he pulls away from me. Reaching his hand back, he rips his shirt over his head and stands in front of me. I reach for the hem of my shirt, but he pushes my hands away.

"I've waited for this for a long time." His voice deep. "So many times, I wondered what you were wearing and wanted to reach under your shirt." His hands caress my smooth stomach. Looking down, I see his hands under my shirt, feel his hands move up to my breasts, my chest going up and down as I wait for the moment his hands cup me. His palms finally cover my breast, and I feel his heat through the lace bra I'm wearing. My nipples peak as my hips move forward to feel his hardness. "Fuck," he hisses when his hand goes to my back and he feels the lace. I cross my arms in front of me, pulling the shirt over my head. I stand there in front of him in my lace bra. Both his hands now go to my breasts, and I look down, seeing his tanned hands on my white skin. "Fits perfectly," he says as he leans down to take a pebbled nipple into his mouth, lace and all. My hand goes to his head while I throw my head back, my senses gone now. He repeats the same thing with the other one. My nipples get harder with the wetness and the cool air. "I have to see you," he hisses and looks like he is going to rip the bra off. I turn around, showing him the back. He groans when he sees the satin crisscross down the middle of my back with a bow tied at the end. He gently pulls the string, undoing the bow, his fingers pulling the satin away till the bra falls to the floor. Turning, I stand in front of him. I look down at myself, my full b cup size, my nipples a dark pink as they pebble. I watch him looking down at me, his hands coming up to cup them in his hands. His eyes never waver from his hands while he rolls each nipple between his thumb and forefinger. The sensation shoots straight to my core, my stomach pulling as it gets tight. My breathing comes in pants as my body wakes for him. "I'm going to fuck these by the time you leave my bed," he says as he pushes them together, and my eyes close, picturing him straddling me as he tit fucks me, my tongue coming out to lick his cock with each forward thrust.

"Jensen," I whisper when he bends his head, taking a nipple into his mouth, this time biting it before rolling it with his tongue. He trails his tongue down the center of my chest to my stomach. Getting on his knees in front of me, he kisses my stomach from left to right, my stomach sucking in. His hands on my hips move to the front of my jeans and one hand roams over the seam of the zipper.

My pussy clenches while I watch his hand go up and down. My hand's in his hair when he finally unsnaps the button, the sound of the zipper louder than we are.

The matching white lace panties are revealed when he pushes my jeans down my hips. His face nuzzles into my pussy as his hot tongue comes out to lick my slit through my panties.

My legs start to shake when I feel him. "Jensen," I plead when my legs finally give out, and I have to sit on the bed. He unties my shoes, throwing them over his shoulder, then pulls my pants off.

He stands up in front of me, my eyes level with his hardness. My hand goes to his button to unsnap it, and then I pull down his zipper. Black Calvin's are the only thing between me and him. My hand cups his cock as I rub up and down, and he throws his head back and moans.

I lean forward as I suck the head in through his Calvin's. The saltiness of pre-cum that leaked out hits my tongue. "No," he says, pushing me down on the bed. He's looking down at me, standing between my open legs.

He kicks off his shoes, and I prop myself on my elbows to watch him the whole time. "Get in the middle of the bed." It's not a suggestion; it's a demand. I turn, getting on my knees, my thong showing my bare ass to him as I look over my shoulder.

His eyes go so dark, they look black. "You play with fire, you're going to get burned." His voice sends a shiver down my body. I lie in the middle of the bed as he crawls to me like I'm his prey. My legs open for him, his hand cupping my breast as he buries his face in my neck, and I feel the weight of him over me. He sucks on my neck as his hunger takes over me. Gone is the soft, gentle Jensen, and in his place is a man who wants to own me.

"I wanted to go slow," he mumbles between kissing, sucking, and nibbling, the whole time his hand rolling my nipple. "I just can't." My legs push back and my hands scratch up his back as the need fills me.

His mouth claims mine this time, his hips rocking into me. My body goes tight, the touches lighting me up everywhere from my head to the tips of my toes. I need him closer; I need more of him.

His hand moves from my breast down my stomach and then his hand slips into my panties. His fingers slip through the folds, the tip of his middle finger grazing my clit, and he easily slips two fingers into me.

I release his mouth to arch my back, throwing my head against the pillow. My hands explore up and down his back while his fingers fuck me, pushing me, making me chase the orgasm. His palm moving side to side on my clit, my stomach gets tight, my hips raise to meet his fingers each time he thrust.

"I'm goi—" I don't say anything because his mouth swallows my words, he swallows my groan, he swallows everything. I come on his fingers, and he doesn't stop; he continues playing my body like a fiddle. My eyes open looking into his. "Jensen."

My fingers trace his lips now to his cheek while he slips his fingers out of me. His weight leaves me, and he kneels in the middle of my legs with his pants still undone. My legs fall to the side, leaving myself open for him.

He brings his fingers to his mouth, cleaning me off

him. "Sweet like honey." He leans over me to open his bedside table and pulls out a box of condoms. "I drove all the way to Walmart for these so no one would see me." He opens the box, ripping it as the condoms fall on the bed. His hand snatches one, but I sit up, my hand going on his.

"When was the …" I look at him. "Last time?"

"The day before Julia left," he answers, and I take the condom from his hand.

"I always used condoms with Eric," I tell him, "and after he died, I got tested. I'm clean." His hands come to my face. "I want all of you."

"Are you sure?" His voice drops to a whisper as I nod. My hands on his hips pull down his pants and his Calvin's. I look down at him, and I blink, my throat going dry. He's the most perfect man in the whole world, and I have him.

"Make love to me," I ask him and lie back down. His hands go to the side of my lace thong as I lift my hips. He slides it down my legs, kissing my knee. He takes off his pants while I watch him. My body's getting ready for him, calling for him. He crawls over me, covering me, kissing me, then returns to his knees. I watch him when he takes his cock in his hand, rubbing the cock head through my folds. He places his cock at my entrance as we both watch him enter me, my body taking him. He pushes all the way inside me, and our moans come out at the same time. "Oh, my god," I say as my hands grip the sheets beside me. He pushes into me over and over, and my legs pull back each time so he can go deeper and deeper. He thrusts his hips, holding my knees back; his thrusts get deeper and deeper, get faster and faster, and then harder and harder.

"You're squeezing the fuck out of me," he hisses, my eyes still watching us as I get wetter and wetter on my way to the finish line. One hand leaves my knee as he puts his thumb into his mouth to wet it and then opens my pussy to find my clit. The wetness from his finger with the wetness of my pussy makes him slide left to right with ease. "You like that, don't you?" he asks, my head nodding while my eyes close slowly. "Your pussy gets tighter every time I talk to you," he says, his thumb now going in circles. "Look at me," he asks. My eyes open as I watch him, the light sheen of sweat covering his body. "Look at your pussy taking me." He looks down at himself. "Swallowing me all in." I watch as I take him, as my body takes all of him. As I push through the finish line, my stomach goes tight, my hips thrusting faster and faster as I grind my clit on his hand. "Come on, Hailey, come on my cock." His dirty mouth pushes me over the edge. My toes curl, and my hands press his ass into me, begging him not to move. He lets me take what I need from him, lets me thrust my hips up as I come over and over and over on his cock. I come so hard I don't hear him say anything, but I don't need to because he grabs my hips to stop me from moving and plants himself all the way in as he comes in me, filling me even more. He falls to the side of me, taking me with him. Our chests both heaving as we try to catch our breath. "I've ..." I look over at him as he starts talking. "No words," he says, closing his eyes. "I think I saw stars." He smiles.

"Good," I tell him. "Because I definitely saw stars with birds floating around." I giggle, and he rolls on his back.

My eyes travel up and down his body, his perfect body, perfect pecs, six-pack to die for, and a cock. "Hailey." I snap out of my trance. "You just licked your lips while eyeing me."

"Did I?" I ask, shrugging. "I was just thinking."

"Yeah, did that thought include a shower?" he asks, climbing out of bed and holding out his hand.

"Does that shower include me getting on my knees?" I kiss his cheek as I walk in front of him, and he swats my ass. "Oh"—I look over my shoulder, his cock now up again—"definitely time to get on my knees." I wink at him as I dash to the shower where he follows me. I definitely get on my knees, but then so does he. When we finally get back to bed, our fingers are all shriveled up and our hair is wet, but we don't give in to sleep just yet. He takes me again, and this time, I do the riding. I end up falling on him as soon as I come, my eyes getting heavy as he rubs my back. I don't know how long I rest because I wake with him sliding into me from behind again. We finish and fall asleep, but throughout the whole night, we reach for each other, never wanting to stop. I don't know how many orgasms I've had when I finally drift off as a light comes into the room from outside.

I'm having the best dream ever. Jensen is all over

me. I feel my nipples being pinched and rolled, my hips moving. I feel his mouth on my pussy. My hands thread into his hair, my eyes slowing opening, and I see it's not a dream. Jensen has his face in my pussy as he eats me. His fingers roll my nipples as his tongue flicks my clit. My hands go on top of his as I mimic his hands. I start to pant, grinding my pussy on his face. I'm about to come when he crawls over me and kisses me, my tongue tasting myself on him. "Morning," he says as he rolls me over, raising my hips and sliding inside me. My chest off the bed, I hold the edge of the mattress while he pounds into me, slowly at first, until I push back on him. He feels my need, and when I throw my head back, he grabs a fist full. One hand holds my hips so tight, I'm going to have his fingerprints, but I couldn't be happier. "Fuck, you're so tight," he says as his balls slap my pussy every time he pounds into me. "Play with your clit," he hisses as his hips push me even farther on the bed.

It doesn't take me long before I'm jumping over the edge where he follows me.

"I can't get enough of you." He kisses my neck when I lie on the bed, tucking my arm under me. "How many times did we have sex last night?"

"Seven," I say, getting up to grab the covers. "Maybe eight," I say, tucking myself in as he scoots over to spoon me from behind. "Hmm," I moan, feeling his chest against me.

"You didn't count the shower," he says.

"Sleep." I yawn. "I'll make pancakes if you let me

sleep for two hours straight." I don't wait for him to answer. His soft snore fills the room, so I turn over and bury my face in his neck and follow him into dream land.

Chapter Twenty-Five

Jensen

I roll over in bed, and my hand lands on the empty place beside me. My body feels like I just ran a marathon, but I can't remember a time I've been happier in my life. I smile when I hear singing coming from the kitchen. Seeing it's only nine a.m., I climb out of bed and grab a pair of shorts. I walk to the kitchen, seeing Hailey in my plaid button-down shirt as she stands by the stove singing and shaking her ass. My cock wakes up to play. I walk into the kitchen, and wrapping my arms around her waist, I bury my face in her neck as I smell her. "Morning, baby." I kiss her as she melts into me.

"Good morning, handsome," she says, flipping the pancake and placing it on the plate. "You need to tell that bad boy I need food before he gets another round." She wiggles her ass, making my bad boy want her even more. She turns in my arms, getting up on her tippy toes to kiss my lips. My hand grabs her ass, and I pick her up, wrapping her legs around my hips.

"Oh, my god." I hear my mother's voice, and my lips pull away from Hailey. I turn to see my mother with her hand against her mouth, her face in shock, and her other hand on Mila's shoulder.

Hailey untangles her legs from my waist, mumbling, "Oh my god, oh my god, oh my god."

"Hailey, did you have a sleepover?" Mila walks away from my mother and climbs on a stool. "And you made pancakes. Nana, can we eat here?"

"Um," my mother says, still looking at us.

Hailey looks like she wishes the floor would eat her up, standing half behind me now. "Did you put chocolate chips in the pancakes?" Mila asks, not even picking up on what is going on.

I turn to Hailey and grab her face, making her look at me. "It's fine." She just shakes her head no, but then nods yes.

"Can I have two please?" Hailey asks, looking around us at the stack of pancakes on the counter.

"Yes. You can," I tell her, then turn to my mother. "Sit down." She just nods.

"I didn't know," Mom says softly. "I had no idea." I get the plate out and pile pancakes on it for Mila. "I'm so sorry." She looks at Hailey.

"Everything is good," I say, putting the plate down in front of Mila. "Hailey, get your coffee." I motion with my head.

"Did you sleep in Poppa's bed?" Mila asks, picking up a piece of pancake with her fork. "Did he make funny noises with his nose?" She mimics me snoring.

"No," Hailey says from beside me as she hides her legs behind the counter.

"So what are you doing here?" I ask my mother, putting a cup of coffee in front of her.

"Mila forgot her rain boots, and we wanted to go hiking a bit." My mother looks at me and then at Hailey. "I should have called."

"Well, that won't happen again," I say under my breath as I drink coffee. We don't say anything while Mila finishes her pancakes. "Go wash your hands and grab your boots by the door," I tell her, watching her walk to the bathroom. "Now, Mother."

She puts her head in her hands. "I'm so, so sorry, Hailey. I swear I had no idea."

"Okay so now that it's out there," I say, looking at my mother and then putting my hand around Hailey's neck and bringing her close to me. "We don't have to keep it a secret."

"Jensen," she whispers, "what about Norma, and …" I don't let her continue; I just kiss her lips and smile.

"I don't care," I say. "I don't give a shit if they plaster it in the papers. I don't care if they take a billboard out on the highway. I don't fucking care," I tell her, and my mother smiles as she watches us.

Hailey's arms go around my waist. "Okay." She leans up, kissing me. "I really, really like your son," she tells my mother, opening her eyes. "Like a lot."

"I can see that," my mother says. "I can also see how happy he is." She smiles at us and then frowns. "I owe your grandmother a hundred dollars."

"What for?" Hailey asks from beside me.

"She called this." My mother points at us. "She called it the minute you stormed into the house and saw Hailey there."

"He hated me." Hailey laughs, looking up at me, her eyes crinkling from the smile.

"I didn't hate you." I hold her closer to me. "I hated the situation."

She shakes her head. "I hated him." I glare at her. "You were such an asshole."

"I wasn't that much of an asshole." I roll my eyes. She pushes me away from her.

"You kicked me out of the house, you basically said 'no wonder my husband left me'." She uses air quotes. "And then I carried your kid in my bare feet, got ten stitches, and you kicked me out of the room." She puts her hands on her hips, and the shirt, even though it reaches her mid thigh, raises a bit.

I shake my head, rubbing my forehead with my hand. "You're right. I was an asshole." I look at her to see that through all this she isn't sad about it or mad about it; she's joking about it. I walk to her, my hands going to her neck. Her hands wrap around my wrists. "Forgive me," I whisper to her; she just smiles and shrugs her shoulders at me.

"Maybe," she says, getting on her tippy toes to kiss me. "You can think of ways to make it up to me."

"Oh really, I can think of a couple," I start saying when my mother yells for Mila, who comes back into the room with her pink rain boots in her hand.

"Give your poppa a kiss," my mother tells Mila as she gets off the chair. "See you two tomorrow." She waves at us, grabbing Mila's hand and walking out.

"Oh, my god," Hailey finally says. "I thought I was going to die."

"Why?' I ask her, smiling. Grabbing some pancakes, I pop them in the microwave to heat them up.

"Your mother knows we've had sex." She points at herself and then me.

I raise my eyebrows, slamming the microwave door after it beeps. "She was bound to find out."

"Really?" She crosses her arms over her chest.

"Really." I pull out a stool, sitting down.

"How so?" Her head tilts to the side, and I'm not sure if this is a test or not.

"Well, since we are now officially dating"—I chew—"it's not going to be a secret."

"You mean just because we've had sex we are officially dating?" Her glare tells me that I should tread lightly.

"No, we were dating long before then." I drink some coffee. "But you kissing me in public yesterday made sure that we are 'officially dating.'" I use air quotes.

"I didn't kiss you; you kissed me." She points at me.

"Don't give a shit who kissed who. It's out there, and I'm not hiding this." I finish eating, bringing my plate to the sink to rinse it off. "I wanted to sit down with Mila and tell her, but considering she found out you slept over, it's too late for that one."

"We aren't hiding this," she whispers, shock on her face as she takes in my words.

"Nope," I tell her, turning to lean against the sink and look at her. "Why do you want to hide it?"

She looks down in thought, and then looks up. "No," she says softly, then loudly again. "No, fuck no." I walk to her. "I'm happy." My fingers start unbuttoning my shirt that she is wearing, and her eyes watch my fingers. I push the shirt open a bit, cupping her breast in my hand. She's fucking perfect; she was perfect before I slept with her, and she is even more perfect now. I roll her nipple between my fingers, causing her eyes to glaze over.

"Before you start something you can't finish, Walker, you'd better go bolt that front door." She removes the shirt from her shoulders, and seeing her standing in my kitchen naked, I can admire her in the light now. She has whisker burns on both breasts. My finger touches them lightly, and she shivers.

"I like this." I trace the little spot. "My mark on you. I've never had the urge to claim someone, for everyone to know that person was mine, but with you, with you"—I shake my head, not sure I can even explain—"I want that. I want everyone to know when you walk down the street that you are Walker's girl."

"Well, unless I walk down Main Street naked, they are going to have to be okay with you kissing and holding my hand in public." She laughs, turning around and walking to my bedroom. "But in the meantime, how about you mark me from behind?" Turning to walk into my room with me following her, by the time we are done, four hours later, we are both out of breath, her ass is pink from my handprint, and my teeth have marked her shoulder. "We need a break."

She looks over. "Where are your t-shirts?"

I point at the closet. "In the closet in the second drawer." My hand on my chest as I try to get my breathing back to normal. That is the best sex I've had in my life. I've had two partners my whole life, Julia and now Hailey, who hands down is the best sex I will ever have. Fuck, she ruined me. "Why?"

"Because I need to sleep, and me naked is too much for you to handle, so I'm going to cover myself." She goes to the closet and comes out wearing one of my t-shirts with my name across it.

I rise to my elbows. "If you think having a shirt on is going to stop me from wanting you"—I laugh—"you are sadly mistaken, especially when you're wearing my shirt."

"Fine, I'll go home," she counters, and my laugh turns into a scowl.

"I'll drag you back here," I tell her, "kicking and screaming. I don't give a shit. Now get in bed so we can nap." I pull the covers off so she can climb in.

She puts her knee on the bed. "Pinky promise you will let me sleep?" Her pinky comes out, and I wrap my pinky around hers.

"Fine." She gets into bed and lies on her stomach. I settle behind her, my legs entwining with hers. "I crossed my fingers." I laugh, my hand roaming up her shirt to hold her breast. "I will still let you sleep."

She wiggles her ass, getting comfortable, and we actually sleep until way after the sun has gone down. Later that night, with her in just my t-shirt, we sit at the island eating frozen pizza with not a care in the world. We spend the night together again, and this time, I wake up to her sucking my cock and taking what she wants. She climbs on me, and as she sinks down, we both groan. By the time we actually get up, we are late.

"What time is lunch again?" She gets on her hand and knees, looking for her other shoe somewhere in the room.

"My grandmother said to be there at noon." I button up my shirt, coming out of the closet and seeing her jeans covered ass. "Fuck." Her head turns my way.

"No. No sex. Found it." She grabs the shoe sitting on the bed and slides it on. "We are on a break from sex."

My eyebrows pinch together. "Who is? I didn't agree to this break." Her head leans back when I stop next to her for a kiss.

"I have to go home and change." She pushes me away, getting up. "Let's go." She walks out of the room to the front door. We get to her house in seconds. Jumping out of the car, she dashes into the house, and I follow her in just as the laughing starts.

"I'm surprised she can walk." Crystal laughs as she stands by the sink in a flowered long-sleeved sundress. "Morning, Romeo." I shake my head, going to fridge and grabbing a water bottle.

"So did you score?" Crystal folds her lips together, looking down the hall to Hailey's bedroom. "If you hurt her, I will fuck you up," she whispers, coming closer to me. "I'm a nurse, so I not only know exactly where to stab you so you bleed out fast, but also where it would hurt the most." I don't say anything because she continues, "That fucktard is lucky he died because if he was alive"—she shakes her head—"he would wish he was dead."

"I'm not going to hurt her," I tell her.

"I know you're not because you love her." She tells me, and I stand there, my mouth suddenly dry, my neck starting to burn. "Don't worry, I won't tell her." She turns to walk away from me. "I'm leaving," she yells. "See you there." The door slams behind her, leaving me looking around.

I love her. I do, completely and utterly love her. I don't know when it happened—fuck that, I know exactly when it happened. When I saw her sitting on the cold beach watching the water, day in and day out. I would take walks, see her, and turn around, then I would spot her sitting and watch her. Watching the same water she watched. Seeing the waves crash into shore, I would gaze ahead at the water, but my mind watched her. I let go of my hatred. I let go of my anger, and I let my guard down.

The night I sat with her, I let go of Julia, and I let go of the future I thought we would have. I let go of the promises I made her … I let go of that part of me. Except with Hailey, that part turned over twice, and it made me see that sometimes no matter how you plan things, how you map it out, life has twists and turns. Sometimes what you think you want isn't what you deserve.

I deserve a woman who will love me and only me. I deserve a woman who wants a life with me, who craves a life with me. Who will put me before her. That is what I deserve. I deserve that perfect love story.

"Ready." I hear Hailey's voice as she walks into the room from her bedroom. Her flowered skirt flows around her legs; her short sleeved white silk shirt tucked in. She is wearing another pair of high heels, but my eyes go to her face.

Her hair pinned back at the side; her eyes shine. There is no sadness there, no emptiness like before. Gone is that girl who first sat on the beach watching the water with all the questions and no answers, and in its place is a woman who is so breathtakingly beautiful my heart skips a beat when she walks into the room. A woman who got her heart ripped out yet is still standing here.

"What's the matter?" she asks me, coming closer to me, her hands going to my waist. "You okay?"

I push her hair from her shoulder to the back, so I can kiss her neck. "I'm fine," I say, and it's not a lie. "I used to watch you."

Her eyes look at me confused. "When you would sit outside, at night, during the day. I used to walk down the beach, see you, and stop." My thumb rubs her pink cheek. "I used to sit and watch the water with you, watch you as you worked through your storm inside."

"I," she says softly, my finger stopping her from talking.

"The first time I saw you, I thought you were so beautiful. But you looked broken; your eyes looked dim, the light gone."

I can't go on without kissing her, so I lean in and kiss her lightly. Her lip gloss stays on my lips. "But each time you left that beach, you got more beautiful, which, to be honest, I didn't think could happen."

Her thumb comes up to wipe my lips. "I was broken." She starts to talk. "I was empty; there was nothing left to me."

"I know, and the sad thing is so was I." I shake my head. "I had the best kid you could ever hope for, I had a successful business, I had a family who loved and supported me, but I was empty."

I smile at her. "I was. I'm not anymore."

"What do you mean?" She looks at me.

"You ... you made me whole again. This thing with us, it started with me wanting to be your friend, it started with two broken people on the beach asking for answers we weren't going to get." I kiss her. "Or we were each other's answers. We were the answers to each other's questions."

"Jensen." A tear rolls down her cheek.

"I love you," I finally tell her, causing her breath to hitch. "I love you." Another tear falls from her eyes. "More than I thought I could love anyone else besides Mila." I smile as the heaviness from before vanishes.

"I don't …" she starts saying.

"You don't have to say anything." I lean in to kiss her lips. "I just wanted to tell you. Now, let's go because we are going to be really, really late," I joke.

"You'd better call and tell them we will be by later." She turns to walk away from me as I stare at her. "I love you." I stand and am about to say something when she holds her hand up. "You had your time; this is mine."

I cross my arms over my chest, watching her look at me. "Okay."

"The worst day of my life was when my husband died because I thought I would die with him. It was a pain that seared through me to my soul. I collapsed in the middle of the hospital to my knees. I asked God to take me too. To take me so I could be with him." She wipes a tear away as anger and fear fills me at the thought of her not being here. "Then the second worst day of my life was finding out that my life was a lie. That everything I thought was real wasn't but a mirage of what life was supposed to be like."

"He was a fool." The words come out.

"For one month, I couldn't sleep until I passed out drunk." She wrings her hands together. "That is how weak I was. I got drunk so I could stop the thoughts, so the memories of us were too blurry for me to remember." Her hand goes to her stomach. "Just thinking back, it makes me sick that I gave him that much more power over me."

"You did what you needed to do to survive," I tell

her as she blinks. The tears falling now, one after another.

"My grandmother came to visit me, showing me a picture of this house. It was the day my life started again. The swings in the front and the back pulled me here." She laughs. "The picture was a bit deceiving since the house was falling apart when I got here, but the minute I stepped out of the car, I started to breathe again. The weight that had crushed my chest for so long was lifting, slowly. I would sit on that swing in the back at night when I couldn't sleep at the beginning, watching the ocean fight its own storm. Seeing the contrast of the calm water out on the horizon and then hearing the waves crash onto the shore. It was my life."

"You are stronger than you think you are," I tell her, making sure she knows.

"I am, and I know that now. I know that because I had to have the two worst days of my life to have the best days of my life to come." Her body goes tall. "I sat on that beach every single day looking for answers, asking questions that no one would be able to answer, because the one person in the world who could answer them wasn't here." She looks down and then up. "Then the answer came to me, you." She sobs. "You, you were the answer all along."

I rush to her, grabbing her face and crushing her lips with mine to swallow the sobs as I hold her. Her hand grips my shirt, holding me as much as I'm holding her. She starts unbuttoning my shirt, and my hands pull her shirt over her head. "I love you," I tell her as I kiss the middle of her chest and feel her heart beating under my lips. "With everything that I am, I love you."

I look up as the tears dry, her eyes sparkling. "I love you more," she whispers. "You, Jensen Walker, are my perfect love story."

Chapter Twenty-Six
Hailey

Six months later.

It's going to be a hot one today, I think to myself as I make my way out to the water. My feet sting from the burning sand as I walk closer to the water. It's going to be a good day. I look at the sun, the heat hitting me right away.

I watch the water wash up the shore, sitting right where the sand gets dark. The beach is still empty because it's just after eight a.m. I look at my tanned legs, thinking about how fast the summer is going to be over. We spend all our time outside. In the pool, in the ocean, my uniform this summer was bikini after bikini. Jensen would groan each time I would buy a new one. He actually bought me twenty one-piece swimsuits. They are sitting in the boxes next to the door with the rest of the boxes of my things. My share of the lease expires today, and in twenty minutes, Jensen will be here to load up my stuff to move me in with him.

We took our time. Well, I took my time. If it was up to Jensen, I would have moved in with him the day he told me he loved me. The day I told him I loved him. The day that turned out to be the best day of my life, but well, since then, there have been many best days, just not as special as that one. I was the one dragging my feet only because I didn't want to just jump. I wanted to ease Mila into it also, but one day when I wasn't there, and she set the table for the three of us, he called to let me know. I did what anyone would do; I hightailed it over there, and we ate dinner together.

"I set the table for us. Silly families always eat together" Mila said as soon as I walked through the door, half out of breath from running down the beach through the sand.

"Thank you for being so helpful," I told her, leaning down to kiss her head. *"Hi there."* I looked over at Jensen, who is taking something out of the oven. I walked into the kitchen; he placed the tray down and approached me.

"Glad you could make it." He kissed me, so naturally, with my hands around his waist.

"I'm going to put some juice boxes on the table," Mila said coming into the room, not even blinking at me hugging her father and us kissing. She didn't bat an eye when she woke up in the middle of the night and climbed into bed with us before I snuck out in the morning.

So now, I sit on the sand, the letter in my back pocket crinkling once I sit. I lean forward and take the letter out of my pocket, looking at the folded white envelope.

I had forgotten about the letter, finding it only when I started packing my boxes. I look down at the envelope, still not sure I want to open it.

I look at the water, seeing the calmness in it, the waves crashing softly today, nothing like when I got here.

I turn the letter over in my hand, my finger sliding under the flap to open it. I pull out the folded white letter and open it up.

Eric's writing gets me right away. Messy, always messy, and printed.

My dear, dear sweet Hailey,

If you are reading this, it means that I didn't have the courage to do this while I was still alive.

I know what you're thinking. Fuck, I don't even know what I'm thinking half the time. But I would like to explain.

The rst time I saw you, it was like my world stopped or got knocked around. You are the most beautiful person I have ever met, inside and out.

I know you are probably wondering why I did what I did, and I wish I had the answer, but I don't. The only thing I know is that I couldn't stay away from you.

I fell in love with two women, and I couldn't

walk away from either of you. I was that sel sh bastard you used to always bitch about. Every single time I came home, I told myself I would tell you the truth, but I just couldn't. I couldn't let you go. When I was with you, I felt alive so alive.

I'm sorry for lying to you I'm sorry for not having the balls to be man enough and deal with whatever it is that would have happened. I'm sorry that in the end you won't remember me with the love and respect you gave me, but with hurt and sadness.

I'm sorry I'm not there with the answers, and I'm even more sorry you have to nd out with this letter. But I want you to know that I loved you. Fuck, I love you with everything I am.

Eric

I wipe the tear from my eye as I fold the letter and put it back in its envelope when I feel him behind me. My strength. "Hi," I say softly as I feel his arms go around me. I lean back into him and move to the side. Laying my head on his shoulder, I feel him rest his chin on my shoulder.

"You read it?" he asks, looking down at the letter in my hand.

"I did," I answer, looking at the water.

"You okay?" The way he asks makes me love him even more. For not asking what it contained, but instead, if I was okay. Me.

"More than okay." Turning my head, I kiss his cheek. He turns his face, looking into my eyes, and leans forward to kiss my lips. "I love you," I whisper, turning to look at the water for a couple of more minutes. I get up, putting my hand out to him. "Let's get me moved out of here." He takes my hand, getting up.

"I think we should have a special sleepover party tonight." He holds my hand as we walk up to the house.

"Is that so, and what type of party is this?"

"Well, I think it should be whip cream, chocolate sauce, and definitely naked." He pulls me to him while I throw my head back and laugh.

"I think we sort of had this party last month. Do you remember Mila asking why you had chocolate syrup in your room by the bed?"

He laughs now. "That was your fault. You wore me out, and I couldn't walk."

I push away from him. "I was sticky the whole day."

We open the back door to the porch, walking into the house. "Happy get out of my house day," Crystal yells from the kitchen. We both laugh, walking through my room, or what will be her room as soon as we walk out.

Crystal decided she isn't leaving this house, so she renewed the lease. "Good morning." I look into the kitchen, seeing her drinking coffee standing there. "Are you going to help us move?"

"Will that make you get out of the house faster?" she asks while I nod my yes with a smile. "Then let's get this shit in the car."

"What time is your roommate moving in?" I hide my smile as she turns and glares at me.

"I can't believe you sold him your share of the lease." Her eyes narrow.

"What did you expect me to do? His house just burned to the ground."

"If Gabe pissed off someone enough that they torched his house, explain to me why it's safe for him to live with me?" she asks, and I shrug my shoulders.

"I wanted to help a friend out."

"Well, next time you get that feeling, call me, and I'll talk you out of it." She points at me. "He gets under my skin," she tells me.

"He definitely is under something," I murmur.

Walking to the stack of boxes, she picks one up and follows Jensen out. I think of her and Gabe, and I hope at the end of all this, they haven't killed each other.

I look around the room, wandering to the fireplace when I notice Crystal put up new pictures. There is one of us two and another of the three of us.

I grab the matches on the mantel, taking a match out and strike it. Grabbing the letter out of my back pocket, I light it on fire. I see the red flames start to eat up the white envelope, the flames burning orange. I set it down in the fireplace and watch the letter turn to ash.

I turn around, walking to the pile of boxes. When I pick up a box and make my way out to my future, I have a spring in my step and a smile on my face.

Epilogue One
Jensen

Six months later

"Dude, you need to chill the fuck out. You're going to wear a hole in the rug," Brody says.

"What if she says no?" I look at him, my heart hammering in my chest.

"She isn't going to say no." Brody gets up. "She's put up with you for this long, so it's safe to say she is in for the long haul. Plus, she looks at you like you hang the moon. She sighs when you kiss her, and she is genuinely happy to see you each time." He walks out of my office.

I walk to my desk, opening the drawer and taking out the brown leather ring case. "Here goes nothing." I put it in my pocket and make my way home.

I walk into the house, and the smell of dinner fills the air. Making my way into the room, I see something that still gets me every single time. Hailey and Mila together. The routine is that Hailey picks Mila up from school, then they do homework together till dinner-time. Then Mila fills Hailey in about everything, and we mean everything, about her day at school.

So it's no surprise that I find Hailey cutting bread while she listens to Mila's story.

"And then someone farted, and they threw up all over the mat." She uses her hands to gesture the act of vomiting.

"Maybe she was sick before?" Hailey looks up, making Mila shake her head. I look around the vast room, taking in the changes since Hailey moved in. The big dark room has light now. The pictures of us scattered around the house. The throw pillows on the big couch and the covers that go with them. Also, the fridge is covered with Mila's schoolwork she brings home, piles and piles of paper. I shake my head. "Hey, girls." I smile, walking to my daughter, and kiss her head, then go around the island to my woman, mine.

Hailey sets the knife down and turns around to greet me with a smile plastered on her face. Her hands go around my neck. "Hi, handsome." My hands bring her close to me while her lips touch mine.

"Dinner's almost done." She turns back around to finish cutting the bread. "I made a pasta bake." She cooks every single night except Saturday; that is our pizza night.

"Great, I'm going to go wash up." I walk to our bedroom, taking in the changes there also. The brown cover is gone, replaced with a light gray one, and more throw pillows that always get tossed on the floor. Pictures of us are everywhere; my girl never misses a picture moment. But my favorite picture of us is the one that Mila took. It is the two of us on the beach, her sitting in front of me, both of us just looking at the water. It's our thing. I take the ring out of my pocket, thinking about how am I going to do this. Putting it in the drawer by my bed, I take a shower before she starts calling for me.

By the time I walk back out, the table is set for the three of us. Mila sits in her chair to my right, and Hailey sits on my left.

"Hailey," Mila shouts, "Poppa is clean."

We sit at the table, telling each other about our day. I hear the vomit story again. Bath time and bedtime go by at a snail's pace. It feels like forever until Mila finally falls asleep. I find Hailey wrapping Christmas presents in our room.

"You know that the gifts will cover most of the tree right?" I ask her.

"I know, but it's our first Christmas sharing a home, and my family is going to be here. *So* I want it perfect." She smiles at me.

"Come with me." I grab her hand and walk to the back door leading to the ocean.

"Where are we going?" she asks surprised when I start walking toward the beach. "Jensen, we won't hear Mila." She stops in her tracks, not moving another step.

"I brought the monitor." I show her. "Now, come on."

We walk down to the sand, and I take in the water. "It's calm tonight," I mention when she sits on the sand, pulling me down by my hand.

"It's getting colder," she mentions as my thoughts are mumbled, and I don't know how to make the first move. I turn to look at her, her hair blowing in the wind. She looks at me, leaning in to give me a kiss. "Love you," she whispers, and I know, I know this is it.

I get up, and she follows my movement. I stand in front of her and then get down on one knee. "Jensen," she whispers.

"I love you," I tell her. "My life was a disaster, like a hurricane came through it, came through me. Left me in ruins. The only good thing I had was Mila." I smile, moving her hair from her face. "But I slowly got up, thought I built everything back, but I didn't. I built the walls, I built the roof, but the foundation, the foundation wasn't there."

"What?" she questions softly.

"When you build a house, it all starts with the foundation. You need a strong foundation to keep everything up."

"Okay." Her hands go to my face.

"So I built this house for me and Mila. Except my foundation was weak. I had none till you."

"Honey." She blinks away tears while smiling.

"You came in and made us stronger; you made us secure. With you, the wind won't knock our house down. The storm will pass over us. I want to dry your eyes when you cry. I want to smile when you smile.

I want to be the one by your side when you have bad days and good days. I want to be by your side even when you want to kick my ass. I want to watch the water with you every day. I want to be the foundation of your world."

"Jensen, you are." She sniffles as she leans forward to kiss me. "You are that and so much more."

"I want to do all that with you as my wife." She gasps.

"Be my wife." I blink away the tears that are now forming. "Please." I reach into my pocket, taking out the box and opening it to show her the simple ring I picked out the day she moved in.

I take her finger and slip the ring on as she looks down at the square diamond ring with a diamond eternity band.

"Say something."

She looks at the ring and then back up. "Yes." Her head moves up and down as the tears flow. "A million times yes."

She gets on her knees, burying her face in my chest as she cries. I hold her until she tilts her head back, the marks of tears all down her cheeks, and her smile bright. "Are you gonna kiss me or not?" I laugh as my mouth claims hers, the wind picking up.

"I think a storm is coming," she says when the sand starts flying up. "Let's go inside." I reach for her hand, not caring about the storm, not caring because I have my foundation. With her, I have everything. With her, I have my perfect love story.

Epilogue Two
Hailey

A beautiful sunny day five months later.

"What do you mean I can't go in there?" I hear Jensen's voice boom from outside our bedroom door, my eyes closed as Darla finishes my makeup. "That's my bedroom."

"Jensen Walker," I hear Heidi say. "Don't make me take out Grandma Delores's whip."

"Mom, my girls are in there, and I want to see them. Mila, open the door for me. Hailey …" I hear Mila giggle from the bed. I open one eye to see my girl sitting in the middle of our bed, reading a book. The puffy dress she is wearing swallows her. My mother has her tucked by her side as she reads to her.

"Poppa is getting angry," Mila tells my mother while she looks up giggling.

Seeing my mother look at Mila with such love makes my heart burst. The day after we got engaged, my family arrived, bearing gifts. With the engagement ring on, I waited to see who would notice it first.

Mom and Dad both came in with their hands filled with gifts, "Are those presents for me?" Mila asked, jumping up and down, clapping her hands.

My father placed them by the tree and then held out his arms for her. She ran to him, and he picked her up. "Santa told me you were a very good girl."

"I was. I help set the table every night," Mila told him.

Nanny then walked into the house. "What a wonderful house, Jensen," she told him as soon as she sat down, "but the car ride was brutal."

"Do you want some tea?" I asked from beside Jensen, his arm around my shoulders.

"I would love some," Nanny said. I walked to the kitchen while my mother and father sat down with Mila. Blake was the only one not able to make it since he was on shift.

I placed the cup of tea on the coffee table in front of them and then finally heard a squeal. "Oh my god, is that an engagement ring. Joanne?" Nanny called my mother who looked away from Mila.

I stood up, finally everyone's eyes on me, the smile not leaving my face even if I tried. I smiled so much my cheeks hurt. I looked down at the ring. "Yes. I agreed to marry him," I told them, their hands flying into the air as they shouted their joy.

"Does this mean that I get to have a grandpop?" Mila asked my father who got tears in his eyes.

"It sure does." He picked her up as he hugged her. "And I have the best looking granddaughter on the play ground."

"Oh dear." I rolled my eyes; she had him wrapped around her finger from the first time they met. She would go for walks with him on the beach holding his hand. She would sit on his lap all the time; when my mother would FaceTime, she would come in and take over the conversation. So that started our first Christmas together, and this year, we were going up to their house.

"He'll get over it, sweetheart." My mother leans down to kiss Mila's head. My family is down for the week. You see, today is my wedding day.

"Okay, you're done," Darla tells me. I stand from the chair and go look at myself in the bathroom mirror. My blond hair is tied at the base of my neck in a messy bun with my bangs swept to the side. My makeup is light. "Now, let's get you in that dress," she says from beside me as the butterflies fill my stomach.

My mother comes into the big bathroom while I step into my lace wedding dress. Putting my arms through, I slip the straps to sit on my shoulders. Darla moves to give my mother room to tie the back. She zips the dress up to my waist and then ties the lace right behind my neck, leaving my back bare. I turn to see myself in the mirror as my mother wipes tears from her eyes. "You look stunning." She grabs me by the waist, pulling me to her. When I called to tell them that Jensen proposed, all my mother did was cry; tears of happiness, she said. You see, Jensen includes my family in everything. Before he even entertained the idea of asking me to marry him, he asked my father and then my mother. My guy is a good one.

"No crying," Darla shouts as my mother nods. Mila comes into the room wearing her cream-colored flower girl dress with a sage belt tied around her waist with a huge bow.

"You look like a princess," I tell her as I stoop down to her level. "I have something for you. Mom, can you bring me the blue box on the dresser?" My mother comes back into the room with the blue box and white ribbon. I take the box in my hand, looking at the beautiful girl in front of me who not only holds a piece of my heart, but who I would also give my life for.

"We are going to wait outside," my mother says. Turning around, she and Darla empty the room, leaving just me and my girl. Yes, mine; she didn't come from me, but she is mine.

"I wanted to ask you something." I smile at her smile as she eyes the box. "Open it."

She grabs the box from me eagerly, untying the bow and letting it fall to the floor. She lifts the lid, taking in the silver chain. "This is called an infinity sign." Her fingers trace the silver eight. "You see how it goes around and around with no ending?" She nods. "I want you to know that this is how much I love you." She smiles at me.

"I love you too." She smiles brightly.

"I wanted to ask you if you would wear it today as a thank you for letting me love you and your dad." She doesn't say anything; she just takes the necklace out and turns around for me to clasp it around her neck.

"Is this like a ring?" she asks turning around. "Like the ring Poppa gave you? He wants to be with you forever."

"Yes, this is just like that." The tears come, and there is no way to stop them.

"I want to be with you forever too," she whispers, coming into my outstretched arms. I kiss her head as I silently thank God for giving her to me. The knock on the door breaks our hug, and Crystal comes into the room.

"You two look like princesses." I see her in her off-the-shoulder sage lace maid of honor dress stopping at her knees.

"Hailey wants to marry me forever," Mila tells her. "Look at my infinity."

She smiles at Mila. "Obviously, she wants to marry you. You're the coolest five-year-old I've ever met." Mila nods her head. "Now, go see Grandma Joanne so she can give you your basket of flowers." She skips out of the room. "That kid has more grandmothers than I could explain." She looks at me as we laugh. "You look amazing." She finally looks at me, coming to me and holding my hand in hers. "There isn't someone else that I would pick for you. There isn't another person on this earth who fits you better than he does." She blinks away tears. "I mean after he stopped being a grade A asshole." We laugh as I pull her to hug me.

"I've never felt like this," I tell her. "My heart is overflowing with love. I loved before"—I take a breath—"or I thought I loved, but this it's different." She doesn't have a chance to say anything because there is a knock on the door and my mother and father open the door.

My mother smiles. "If we don't get you out there right now, I think Jensen is going to get a bulldozer and make a hole in that wall." I smile and silently laugh because he probably would.

"Okay, let's go get me married." I grab my bouquet of white and green wildflowers.

I walk out to the back where I see the altar on the beach for the first time. White chairs line the aisle, all of them filled with everyone we know. I take in all the love that is on that beach. Mila comes out to me. "I got my flowers to throw down."

"Okay, let's do this," I tell everyone as I spot Nanny and Grandma Delores sitting side by side. The music starts as I look up and see Jensen walk to the altar at the end of the aisle, flowers all around it. He stands there in his beige linen suit, white shirt with no tie. He stands there with his hands crossed in front of him as Gabe and Brody stand to his side, wearing the same thing but with just vests and no jackets.

Darla walks down the aisle first, with Crystal following her. I look at my parents, who hold hands. "If you don't mind, I want to walk down the aisle with Mila." I reach for her hand, smiling. They nod their head as they walk each other down the aisle. When "Bless the Broken Road" starts playing, I squeeze Mila's hand before we start down the aisle. My eyes find Blake's as I look at him and his family. His wife's eyes brim with tears as I subtly nod at her. I start my walk down the aisle, my eyes never leaving Jensen's as he wipes away his tears. I pass the rows of chairs that include our family, aunts, uncles, and all of my friends.

When I get to the altar, Jensen grabs my face, kissing me softly. "We haven't gotten to that part, son," the officiant says while everyone laughs. Mila walks over to sit with my mother and father, climbing on my father's lap.

In the middle of the beach, with the water calm as soft waves hit the sand, we promise to love, honor, and cherish each other. I promise Jensen and Mila that I will love them forever. When he slips the eternity band on my finger, my heart fills even more than I thought was possible and a soft sob escapes me. I slip his simple gold band on his finger, and he pulls me to him, not caring if it's the time or not. I kiss him, wrapping my arms around him, as our family and friends all clap and holler behind us. "I love you," I tell him when he releases my lips.

He turns to face everyone, his hand grabbing mine as he lifts them in the air. "She's mine, people." The crowd goes wild as I laugh with my whole heart.

Some nine months later

I walk on the beach, my feet sinking in the sand, and a notepad in my hand. I sit down in the middle of the empty beach as the sun rises in the distance, the water slowly coming to life. As the waves crash faster and faster, I pull the pen out and start my letter.

Dear Eric,
It feels like it's been forever since I last thought of you.
I hope you are looking down and know I'm happy. I don't think I've ever been this happy in my life.
I have a husband who I would not only die with, but I would die for. I have a beautiful daughter named Mila. My name now on her birth certificate as her mother.

I wanted to tell you that I forgive you. I forgive you for everything. I have to forgive you because of you, I got my everything. I got my perfect life.
Hailey Walker

I stop writing as I rub my swollen stomach while my son kicks to let me know that today he will be meeting me. I look at the water, a lone bird chirping in the distance. Coming closer and closer, he soars into the sky, and it almost looks like he's watching me. I get up, the lightness overtaking me as I walk back to my house, to my family.

Books By Natasha Madison

Something Series
Something So Right
Something So Perfect
Something So Irresistible

Tempt Series
Tempt The Boss
Tempt The Playboy
Tempt The Neighbor–2018
Heaven & Hell Series

Hell and Back
Pieces of Heaven
True Love Series
Pefrect Love Story
Unexpected Love Story
Broken Love Story

Novellas
Cheeky
Until Brandon

Madison Rose Books
Only His

Acknowledgments

Every single time I keep thinking it's going to be easy. It takes a village to help and I don't want to leave anyone out.

My Husband: I love you, I don't tell you enough. Thank you for letting me sit in bed most of the day writing, and for not busting my chops when I don't cook. Oh wait you do!

My Kids: Matteo, Michael, and Erica, Thank you for letting me do this. Thank you for being proud of me, I love you honey bunches and oats!

<u>Crystal</u>: My hooker and bestie. What don't you do for me? Everyone needs someone like you in their corner and I am so blessed than you chose to be in mine. I can't begin to thank you for the support, love and encouragement along the way.

<u>Rachel:</u> You are my blurb bitch. Each time you do it without even reading this book and you rocked it. I'm so happy that I ddin't give up when you ignored my many messages.

<u>Meghan:</u> I'm so so proud to call you my friend. Thank you for making me make that list, and making me see I can actually achieve it.

<u>Jamie & Sarah:</u> Thank you for being in my corner, and always having my back.

<u>Lori:</u> I don't know what I would do without you in my life. You take over and I don't even have to ask or worry because I know everything will be fine, because you're a rock star, I'm also scared of that whip!

Denise: The hole finder. I can't put into word how honored I am that you took Max and made me make him even more Epic! I can't wait to bring Denise to life!

Melissa: My cover girl, I have more covers than stories, but I know you won't let me stop. Thank you for sending me covers while I sleep so I don't yell at you before you go to bed. I love you.

Beta girls: Teressa, Natasha M, Lori, Sandy, Yolanda, and Carmen, Yamina. For three weeks I bombarded your messages with chapters and you ate it up. Thank you for holding my hand, telling me when things sucked and for being by my side.

Madison Maniacs: This little group went from two people to so much more and I can't thank you guys enough. This group is my go to, my safe place. You push me and get excited for me and I can't wait to watch us grow even bigger!

Mia: I'm so happy that Nanny threw out Archer's Voice and I needed to tell you because that snowballed to a friendship that is without a doubt the best ever!

Neda: You answer my question no matter how stupid they sound. Thank you for being you, thank you for everything!

Julie: Thank you for taking my book with all it's mistakes and making it pretty, or as pretty as it can be.

BLOGGERS. THANK YOU FOR TAKING A CHANCE ON ME. You give so much of yourself effortlessly and you are the voice that we can't do this without.

My Girls: Sabrina, Melanie, Marie-Eve, Lydia, Shelly, Stephanie, Marisa. Your support during this whole ride has been amazing. I can honestly say without a doubt that I have the best Squad of life!!!!

And Lastly and most importantly to YOU the reader, Without you none of this would be real. So thank you for reading!

Made in the USA
Middletown, DE
04 September 2023